Hidden hearts

Randel, Tara

HIDDEN HEARTS

HIDDEN HEARTS

•

Tara Randel

AVALON BOOKS
NEW YORK

47740

PRINTED IN THE UNITED STATES OF AMERICA
ON ACID-FREE PAPER
BY HADDON CRAFTSMEN, BLOOMSBURG, PENNSYLVANIA

To Megan and Kathryn, the best daughters this Mom could ask for.

To Randy—without you, I couldn't have told this story. Thanks for your unending support and love.

To Paula Decker—a pleasure to work with. Thanks for your insight and talent for drawing out the best in an author.

Chapter One

Teri Price rubbed tense fingers against her throbbing temples. The alarmed tone of her assistant's message echoed in her mind—*the complaints have started again.*

Why not? During peak season with the hotel filled to capacity! She tried not to worry over the earlier phone conversation with her boss, the general manager. He'd reminded her, in none-too-friendly terms, that he expected the West Wind Hotel and Resort to be running in shipshape fashion for the annual review. She assured him that his wishes would be carried out to the exact order, but deep down she dreaded the next catastrophe that would make or break her career.

Her assistant, Tom Preston, interrupted her depressing thoughts. "Mr. Bishop is on his way up to speak with you," he said before scurrying from the office, leaving the door ajar.

1

Great. Just what I need.

Teri bristled at the thought of him. Jack Bishop, the bane of her professional existence. Bothersome? Most certainly. Tenacious? Absolutely. Handsome? Unfortunately for her, the most attractive man she'd ever met. It irked her that he got under her skin so easily.

Hotels, Inc., the parent company she worked for, hired Jack's firm, Champion Safeguards, to reorganize the hotel security system. The current security staff—a bit lax in her opinion—needed fresh insight into the meaning of surveillance, protection, and, well, hard work. She informed corporate about her concerns and promised to whip the staff into shape. The next thing she knew, Jack Bishop landed on her doorstep.

She didn't need his help. Didn't want his help. But she'd been stuck with him for a month now.

Closing her eyes, she mentally prepared for the exchange with Jack. To her dismay, her stomach dipped as it always did in his presence. She shook her head, determined not to let hormones dictate her response to that exasperating man.

As if conjuring up Jack by her thoughts alone, she heard heavy footsteps heading her way from the main foyer. Standing behind her desk, she forced a smile, ready to face him. She had the home court advantage: her office, her turf.

"This is no way to run a hotel," Jack declared as he barged into the room, all male and itching for a fight. He closed the door with a heavy thud and stood partially shadowed by the late afternoon light streaming through the window. As he leaned into a beam of direct sunlight, his tousled blond hair gleamed with sun-bleached highlights. Chocolate brown eyes held a hint of annoyance. She swallowed. No man had a right to look so good.

His curt words cut into her wandering thoughts.

"First," he continued, "remodeling the Jacaranda wing becomes top priority to management, then the contractor suddenly disappears. He promised to be back in a week or so, but he's a no-show. We have nothing now. No contractor, no permits, no renovations. I've heard that bureaucratic wheels turn slowly, but this is ridiculous." His dark eyes challenged her. "And I just heard from the front desk that we've had another complaint about the noises. The third this week."

Teri sighed. She was well aware of the complaints and the AWOL contractor. "It's your firm's job to find the cause of those strange noises, and it's my job as assistant general manager to assure the guests that everything possible is being done to correct the problem. You, Mr. Bishop, have not found the source of their complaints."

One sandy eyebrow arched over his eye. "Hey, I'm not the one facing the top brass for a job review."

"Nice of you to jog my memory," she muttered, turning away from the scowling security expert to gaze out her office window. Seagulls swooped toward the water as children scampered on the sand, chasing the elusive birds. "West Wind will pass the review with flying colors."

It had to—Teri's future with the hotel chain depended on it. If the Clearwater Beach resort hotel failed to pass muster, she could kiss her promotion to Paris good-bye. And, if she screwed-up again, most likely her career would go with it. "You know, this won't look good for your firm either, Jack."

"Good point." He was silent for a long moment, then spoke hesitantly. "I propose we work on this problem together."

"I work alone," she announced as she spun around, her fingers gripping the edge of the desk.

"So do I, but this time we're going to have to work alone, together."

She ground her teeth.

This man had an innate self-assurance that made those around him seek out his presence. He'd been at West Wind for one month, but this was the man her staff politely deferred to. The man who stopped women in their tracks and didn't seem aware of it. The kind of man that guests warmed up to when he made rounds.

In the short time he'd been at this property, Jack seemed to shadow her in his looming presence. She'd quickly learned that a year ago he'd been employed by her parent company before venturing out to start his firm, so many of her employees already knew him. They liked him and worked well together. She realized the staff needed time to adjust to her, to realize that although she'd been here a mere six months, she was in charge. But her patience was running thin. *She'd* come here to run this hotel, not Jack.

Teri cleared her throat. "What do you suggest *we* do?"

Jack tilted his head, his dark gaze narrowing. "I suggest *we* stake out room 213."

"Can't do that. That suite is booked until the first week of April."

"Since this is only the beginning of February, you can find alternative accommodations before your guests arrive. We have to find the source of those noises coming from that suite."

Oh sure, Teri thought. Just tell her guests that the reservations they made a year ago are no good. She shook her head. "Impossible, Jack. We'd only receive more complaints. I won't risk it."

Jack smiled, a devilish gleam lighting his eyes. He rested his hip against the side of her desk, folding his arms over his chest. "There's a rumor starting, you know."

Teri lifted her chin, worried by his amused expression. She could handle gossip, she had before. But still, her stomach churned in apprehension. "And just what would that be?"

"I've heard the staff say room 213 is haunted."

"Haunted!" She laughed in relief. "You've got to be kidding."

He nodded.

"That's absurd!"

"Well then, you try to explain the strange sounds in that room."

She leaned back against the window sill, her fingernails rapping a staccato beat on the ledge. She had to squelch this crazy rumor. With this new pressure from Jack, her head started to throb. The calypso music flowing from a hidden speaker system didn't help. She needed silence to think over this crazy turn of events.

"Jack, let me think about this. I'll get back to you."

"Teri, you know we have to deal with this now," he said, the deep timbre of his voice washing over her. "You can't sweep this under the rug and hope it goes away. We have to get on the problem now before the contractor returns to finish the renovations—*if* he does, that is." He paused. "Besides, this isn't Daytona Beach."

At his words, a painful breath escaped her. How did he find out about her troubles in Daytona? Someone at corporate must have told him. How dare he throw that in her face now!

She pulled up her five-foot-six frame and squared her shoulders, determined to present a strong front through this latest battle of wills. "What happened in Daytona is between me and corporate."

He threw up his hands. "Hey, I didn't mean to touch a nerve. Look, we still have suite 213 to worry about."

"And how do you propose we stake out a booked suite?"

He leaned toward her, speaking in a low voice as if he had a secret to share. "I overheard the Meyers having a fight, and found out they're checking out of 213 tomorrow morning. The room will be vacant until Friday afternoon. That gives us two nights to stay in the suite and investigate the noises when we hear them."

"You're snooping on the guests?"

"It was kind of hard to miss. They were standing in the foyer at the time."

She silently fumed, then his earlier words dawned on her. He wanted them together? In the suite? Alone?

Surely she hadn't heard him correctly. She wiped damp palms over the straight blue skirt of her lightweight suit. "*Us?*"

"Yes, us." He smiled, a lopsided grin that set her stomach flip-flopping again. "I'd think as the head honcho around here you'd want to be in on the investigation firsthand."

Her voice cracked. "Just the two of us?"

"The staff will be on duty, no need to worry." His smile disappeared, an accusatory tone edged his voice. "Are you afraid to be alone with me?"

"Of course not," she sputtered. "How could you think that?"

He rubbed his chin, brushing over the start of a stubbly five o'clock shadow. "Methinks thou dost protest too much."

"You can think what you like," she snapped, angry at his goading, angry at her reaction to him. "I'll meet you in room 213 Wednesday night at nine o'clock. Sharp."

"There's another thing," Jack said, good humor returning to his tone.

"Now what?" She focused on some papers on the desk, afraid to hear his answer.

"I'm going to the building department first thing in the morning. I think the contractor left with the blueprints, so I want a copy of the originals. Maybe they'll give us a clue to help pinpoint the noises."

Teri swallowed her mounting anger. *Here he goes again, taking over.* "No need. I'll send one of the staff. The hotel and its day-to-day operations fall under my responsibilities, so once we have a copy, I'll look it over." She felt calmer now, back in control. "We should also get a copy of the contractor's permits. I can't find any records, either."

Jack parked his hands on his lean waist. "What do you know about permits?"

Not much, she thought, but winged it. "Enough to ask if they were applied for and received."

He shifted his weight from one foot to another, considering her words. Finally, he said, "We should both go."

"Both of us? Is that necessary?"

"It is if we want to share information."

She considered his position in this mini drama and realized that his reputation was on the line, too. The job he did at this hotel would determine the future of his security firm. He needed answers as much as she did, even though she hated giving him so much control. And like it or not, a small voice kept nagging at her that maybe, just maybe, she might need Jack's help in this matter.

"If nothing pressing comes up, I'll meet you there."

"Whatever, but I'll be there." He strode from the room, exuding a self-confidence that Teri found as attractive as she did annoying. She should learn how he channeled his energy. It might help her win the loyalty of her employees. And maybe steer her wavering position back in control.

Teri straightened her desk and hurried out to the foyer to make her rounds. Her sensible shoes clicked across the fine Italian marble. Nodding at the employees working behind the ornate registration desk, she stopped to adjust a floral arrangement set on an antique wall table. With a satisfied nod of her head, she stepped back to observe her small touch.

A couple strolled by, and Teri smiled brightly, inquiring about their stay, asking if they needed anything. Rule number one of hotel management: never let them see you sweat.

Especially when thoughts of spending time alone in a vacant room with Jack Bishop had her perspiring.

The rich smell of coffee drew her to the reception area, where she stopped to pour herself a cup before heading to the large recreation room. She smiled, mentally patting herself on the back.

When she'd arrived, this room had been a jumbled mess of games, books and magazines. Enlisting the help of her assistant, they managed to find some cozy furniture in storage, along with a forgotten pool table. Redecorated, the room invited guests to relax and enjoy themselves.

Two laughing teen-aged girls opened the large rear door leading to the pool, allowing a chilly winter breeze to slip in and swirl around the room. The crash of waves sounded briefly before the door closed. Teri breathed in, filling her lungs with the soothing smell of salty air.

"Enjoying the view, Miss Price?"

Teri spun around to face Martin Pressman, a representative of the local historical society, busy gathering information for some upcoming project.

In his late sixties, his eyes held a lively sparkle, and his sparse, though unruly, hair still held a bit of brown mixed with gray. His shoulders hunched over a bit, but he glowed with good health. In the short time Teri had known him, he'd come to remind her of her beloved father.

"It's beautiful here."

He walked over to stand beside her. "You should have seen it fifty years ago. The island was unspoiled." He sighed. "That was before tourism took over. But I suppose this is a sign of progress."

"What a shame."

"Yes, it is." He pointed at the guest buildings that fanned out from the main structure they stood in. "My father helped build the wings, back in the twenties. I must know more stories about this hotel than any person alive."

An idea popped into Teri's head. "Would you mind taking a few minutes to talk to me?"

"Any excuse to sit with a lovely lady."

Teri led them to a plush couch and motioned for him to take a seat. She waited until he leaned back in the cushions before voicing her question. "What can you tell me about the history of the hotel? Especially the Jacaranda wing."

He rubbed his chin. "My father came to work here as a handy man. West Wind was a small family-owned hotel back then. He joined the construction crew when they decided to make the hotel bigger. I was born just as they finished the last building. My father continued to work here until he retired, and I worked here, as well."

"That sounds like me and my dad. After Mom died, we worked at one hotel or another. I ended up doing odd jobs until I was old enough to work the desk."

"Your father must be proud of you."

Memories brought unbidden tears, stinging her eyes. "Dad passed on three years ago." She took a breath and forced a shaky smile. "I followed in his footsteps. But instead of odd jobs, I worked my way to assistant GM."

Martin reached out, his bony fingers covering hers. He trembled, but the warmth of his touch soothed her. "Believe me, he is proud of you."

She swallowed the lump in her throat. This was no way for a trained manager to behave. After all, she'd made her choices, choosing a career over marriage and family. It was lonely sometimes, but it was all she had.

She shifted back to professional mode. "I'd really like to hear more of your stories. We've had a few problems around here, and I'm hoping you can help."

"You mean about the ghost sounds."

Her eyes opened wide with surprise. "Rumors *do* travel fast around here."

"That's always been the way." He placed his arm

on the armrest to steady himself as he stood. "Gossip makes the small world of this hotel go round."

Teri also stood. "That doesn't make me feel any better."

"Don't worry. No one ever gets the facts right."

A slow smile spread over her lips. "But I'll bet you do."

He nodded. "When you're ready, give me a call at home. I'd be happy for you to come out to my place." He whispered behind his hand. "I've had a lot of free time since I've retired."

"I'd love to," she replied, touched by the first real invitation she'd had since arriving here.

"Good. I'll expect your call." He ambled from the room. She followed, and as she turned the corner of the lobby, she glimpsed Jack leaving the building. His determined stride suggested a man with a specific destination.

She watched his fluid movements until he disappeared from sight. Then her smile grew bigger, her mood soared. With Martin on her side, she'd have information Jack didn't.

For the first time, she had the upper hand.

Chapter Two

J ack glanced toward the glass door as he lounged in a chair of the county building, wondering which employee Teri would saddle him with. Yesterday when he told her he intended to come here, he didn't think she'd take him up on his small dare. But he couldn't help baiting her anyway. Her dedication to her job bordered on extreme.

He checked his watch and frowned. Ten minutes late. Miss Persnickety wouldn't like this at all.

He stood, ready to get on with the job, when Teri burst into the reception area like a whirlwind. He tried to hide his surprise at seeing her, but knew he failed when she lifted her chin in defense and stopped before him.

"Do you think this will take very long?" she asked as she caught her breath.

"What are you doing here?"

She brushed a stray lock of toffee brown hair from her green eyes. "I'm short staffed. I can't afford to send Tom—he holds the front desk together—and I suddenly realized you were waiting for someone to meet you. So, despite what I said yesterday, I decided to come over."

He couldn't hold back a grin. "I could have handled this on my own."

She squared her shoulders. "Like you said, we should work on this problem together. I may be able to help you in some way."

"Yeah, you can carry the blueprints back to the hotel."

As she glared at him he had to control the urge not to laugh. He really enjoyed her show of spirit. Maybe there was more to Teri than work and only work.

"I hope we're next." She shook her wrist to turn the watch face around. "I always get antsy when I'm away from the hotel too long. Tom has everything under control, but I'm on duty and I should be there."

"This won't take too much longer. Besides, you're here on hotel business. Don't worry so much."

When the woman behind the counter called him, Jack took Teri's arm. "That's us." A middle-aged woman with graying hair stood patiently waiting for them to state their business.

"We'd like the original blueprints for the West Wind Hotel," Jack explained. "And upgrades made from about 1920 to the present, including recent requests for remodeling permits."

The woman pushed a form toward them. "If you'd fill this out, I'll locate those plans for you."

Jack pushed the paper toward Teri. "You want the honors?"

"Sure. It'll give me something to do." She rummaged around in her purse and extracted a pen.

"Do you always have to be doing something? Don't you ever relax just for the fun of it? Sit back on the beach and watch a sunset, or lay by the pool with a good book?"

She stared at him as if he'd just sprouted horns. "I don't have time for fun. There are only so many hours in the day and I'm too busy to just lay around."

"Don't you ever take a day off?"

She looked annoyed for a moment. "Of course I do."

"When was your last day off?"

Teri opened her mouth, then quickly closed it. Her eyebrows pulled over a wary expression, unsuccessfully hiding her pique. The small gesture wasn't wasted on him

"You can't remember, can you?" he asked, satisfaction lacing his voice.

She colored brightly, then turned her attention to the form in front of her. Jack chuckled at her stall tactics.

"I think you should consider taking a day off sometime soon. You know, to shake off that I'm-a-workaholic syndrome."

Teri huffed. "I like my work."

"Yeah, but all work and no play . . ."

"Makes *Jack* a dull boy," Teri finished, "not me."

"That remains to be seen."

He was rewarded with another scowl in his direction. She filled out the form and made faces at him with practiced ease. He got a reaction all right, but having her peeved at him was not his intention.

The woman took the completed form, asked a few questions about the hotel, and returned with the sought-after blueprints, laying them on the counter. "I checked on those permits you asked about. There have been no applications from any of the local contractors for West Wind."

Teri turned to Jack, surprise mirrored on her face. "That can't be. I'm sure I saw a permit posted before the remodeling work started at the hotel."

He nodded. "And I saw the site-supervisor looking over the job. One subcontractor even came in, ready to tear out a wall."

"I'm sorry, I can only tell you what I know, and there were no permits applied for. Is that all you need?"

"For now." He looked at Teri. "I don't like this."

She nodded.

"Let's head back to the hotel. I'll start looking over the blueprints."

Jack strode into his makeshift office at West Wind to find the small room filled with employees. His domain always seemed to have its share of people milling in and out. Ed Raven, the in-house chief of security, sat at Jack's desk, his worn sneakers resting on the blotter. Tom, Teri's assistant, stood in the corner, while a new guy from maintenance reclined in a chair placed before the desk.

"What're you guys doing here?" Jack dumped the roll of prints by Ed's sneakers, then swiped at his feet. With a jerk, Ed scrambled to set his feet on the ground.

"We're talking about the female employees." Ed snickered and pushed up his glasses.

Jack opened the plans and spread the papers across the desk. Women were the only topic of conversation Ed indulged in. He did his job, Jack had no complaints, but everyone knew about Ed's social life—or lack thereof.

"Actually," Ed said, "we were placing bets."

Jack raised an eyebrow. "On company time?"

"It's not like that. We wondered if anyone here had the nerve to ask Teri Price out."

Jack straightened so quickly that the pages snapped back into the roll. He searched the faces of all three men, looking for signs of dementia. Instead, each held a sheepish expression. "Why Teri Price?"

Ed shrugged. "She's not exactly the warmest woman around, so we figured it would have to be a special guy to get her motor going, if you get my drift."

Unfortunately, Jack understood him all too well. "*Our* Miss Price?" he asked again. Something close to jealousy pricked at him, which was ridiculous, since he'd only known the woman for a month. He tried to force the unwelcome feeling away, but it lingered as the conversation progressed.

Tom stepped forward. "Look, she's not that bad. She's only been here a short time. Maybe we should give her a chance."

Ed's eyes widened behind thick lenses. "Last week you were complaining about what a tyrant she is. Why defend her now?"

Jack looked over at Tom. *Yeah,* he thought, *why come to her rescue now?*

Tom rubbed the back of his neck and paced. "I don't know. I just don't think she'd appreciate being the subject of a bet."

Jack leaned back against the wall, crossing his arms over his chest.

Ed waved his hand. "It doesn't have to be a real bet, but c'mon. What guy is gonna ask her out if he's afraid of her? You have to admit, she can be pretty tough."

The new employee looked pointedly at Jack. "How about you? Your job is pretty important. Like hers. Maybe she's one of those women who's big on equality."

Ed nearly jumped out of the chair. "That's perfect! The girls in this place fall all over themselves to get you to notice them. She'd be crazy to say no."

Jack frowned. He could have sworn she felt uncomfortable around him. Of course, he hadn't given her much of a break since he arrived. Maybe he should cut her some slack. Then she'd lighten up on the staff. But ask her out? Bet or no bet, that took them into a whole new realm, one he wasn't sure he wanted to step into.

Behind her stiff, by-the-book attitude, Jack noticed an attractive woman. He wouldn't admit it to the guys, but the thought of getting to know her better had crossed his mind. He'd just been too busy to dwell on the idea. Maybe it was better to leave well enough alone.

Jack shook off his thoughts. "I think you guys have too much time on your hands." He moved back to the blueprints, ready to settle down and study the layout.

Ed wouldn't be put off. "Ask Miss Price out as a sign of solidarity to your brothers in the dating war."

Jack cringed at the idea, and started to tell Ed so when the phone rang. He snatched the receiver before Ed had a chance. "Bishop here."

He nearly groaned out loud when he recognized the voice on the other end. Whenever he spoke to his mother he had the same reaction—wishing he was an orphan.

For long minutes he listened to his mother's terse message, without interrupting, then lowered the receiver into the cradle, forcibly grinding his teeth. If guilt had a name, it would be spelled m-o-t-h-e-r.

"So," Ed continued, as if never interrupted, "you ask Miss Price out—"

"Don't push it," Jack warned, then mentally counted to ten. "Why don't you guys get out of here so I can get some work done?"

They scrambled out as Jack settled into the chair behind his desk. He rolled out the pages and held the ends down with the telephone and a college football trophy. Fifteen minutes passed before the ringing phone interrupted him again.

"Bishop here."

"Hello, Jack. How are things?"

At the sound of the voice on the other end, Jack leaned back in his chair. He rubbed his eyes with thumb and fore finger. "Running smoothly."

"And Miss Price?"

Since he'd arrived, the general manager, Don Kramer, called him frequently to check on Teri's performance. Jack was always forthright, but today he had a nagging feeling he shouldn't mention the problem with the noisy wing. "Like I said, sir, everything is just fine."

"Wonderful. Oh, by the way, your first report on Miss Price is quite thorough. Keep up the good work."

"Thank you."

"When can I expect another?"

Jack glanced down at his desk, to the legal pad where he'd scribbled some notes. "I'm working on a report now."

"I'll be waiting for it."

Kramer continued with his instructions and by the time Jack hung up, the hairs on the back of his neck were tingling. In the years he'd worked for the corporation, he'd run into Kramer at different properties and he always had the same impression of the man. Kramer reminded him of a snake oil salesman, oozing with compliments as long as you bought into his agenda, which in this case focused on Teri.

He flexed his shoulders, trying to work out the tension. As much as Teri bugged Jack, she seemed one hundred percent committed to her job. But whatever he might feel about her was nothing compared to the loyalty he gave to the company that had taken him in.

When he was down on his luck, Marcus King, CEO of Hotels, Inc., had taken a chance on hiring him. Even though Jack's last job with a private investigation firm had turned out badly, Jack never let Marcus down, doing the best job he was capable of for four years. When he decided to strike out on his own, Marcus supported the decision. Jack owed Marcus and the corporation, and would do what he was asked.

He hated the idea of doing Kramer's dirty work, but he'd done worse in his career.

Thoughts of how he'd tried to please his parents by taking a job with a local PI agency haunted him. He'd worked for the firm for two years before he headed his own surveillance team. A client thought his wife was cheating on him and wanted proof. Jack was inexperienced in domestic problems and his boss knew it, but he found out the woman was cheating, filed his report, and a week later the guy murdered his wife. Jack quit right then.

He rubbed his neck, trying to relieve the tension and the memories. His gaze went to his prized college football trophy holding down the blueprints, and he grinned. He'd played ball with Marcus's son, which was why he'd taken a chance on Jack. Marcus thought he had potential, even if his family didn't.

He'd become persona non grata at the Bishop home.

So he stayed away and hoped one day he'd get over the guilt that never quite went away. So far, no luck.

His thoughts strayed back to Teri. He knew she'd made a mistake at her last job. In some way they were kindred spirits, even though she had no clue about his past. If he was lucky, she'd never find out.

He picked up the legal pad and read his notes about Teri. Efficient in the day-to-day handling of hotel affairs. Pleasant to guests. At times short with the staff, putting them on the defensive.

He lifted his pen to cross out the last sentence, then hesitated. Hey, he only recorded what he'd observed. Nothing more, nothing less.

So when those pesky flashes of conscience nagged at him, he quickly turned it off. He couldn't afford to lose his perspective here. Hotels, Inc. had hired him to revamp the security system at West Wind. Kramer worked for the corporation, so even though he didn't like the guy, he figured Kramer had his reasons for watching Teri. Jack didn't like his methods, but he wouldn't dispute them.

He turned to his computer and clicked on a word processing program. With determined strokes, he typed his second report. He started with Teri's good points, hoping to cancel out the negative. Overall, she did well, except with the staff. Hadn't he experienced her commitment to the job firsthand in their heated discussions about the hotel? It was almost as if she was afraid to be feminine, as if somehow, that attribute would take away her authority. Whatever her reason, it affected the employees, and he included that fact in his report.

He saved the file before printing out a copy. He reached for the paper, questioning his objective as he proofread. Although uncomfortable with Kramer's demands, he had his firm to consider. His performance here would influence future contracts. He had to keep that in mind, as he always did when making decisions for Champion Safeguards.

Ever efficient, he tore his notes from the legal pad to run through the shredder. He found a large envelope to mail the report, printing the address in bold letters before placing the envelope in his briefcase. Lastly, he make a mental note to visit the post office. Now finished, he left his office, more than ready to make his rounds.

And if his still, small voice started acting up, he'd just ignore it. He'd done that plenty of times in his life.

Chapter Three

The late night wind howled outside as Jack studied the building plans spread out before him. Yesterday, after Kramer's call, he'd left his office and never got a chance to read them. Now, alone in the quiet suite, waiting for Teri to arrive, he wanted a better idea of the layout of West Wind. Placing palms down on the desk, he leaned forward, eyes intent on the sheets before him.

The hotel was oddly shaped. The main building housed reception, a nautical-themed cocktail lounge and elegant four-star restaurant. Guests could also enjoy a spa and exercise room.

Three separate wings contained the guest rooms, appropriately called Jacaranda, Gardenia, and Magnolia. The names carried an aura of the old south. Each wing had five stories, all angled to have a water view from a small balcony. No matter which room a guest stayed in, a romantic Florida sunset or bright morning sunrise could be seen. Actually, the hotel was an architectural wonder in the year it had been built.

From what he could see, the Jacaranda wing had been constructed in the late 1920's. Since then, major renovations had modernized this portion of the building, but problems had always plagued work on the first floor. The room he stood in, 213, lay one story above the closed lower wing, vacant until the contractor returned with his permits and workers.

So where were the noises coming from?

When Jack first arrived at the hotel, he'd scoured the entire building, and recently investigated the closed-off area. Even then he wondered why potential revenue producing rooms were left idle. He'd called Kramer and received this vague answer, "These rooms have always been an architectural problem, and they'll stay empty until renovations are complete."

It was an incredibly vague response, but his job was security, not in-house decisions made by corporate managers. So he kept the area off-limits to the guests, and periodically inspected the wing himself to make sure nothing seemed out of order.

He stood to stretch, then checked his watch. Miss Uptight Manager should arrive shortly. If she said nine o'clock sharp, she meant it.

Sauntering to the window, he slid the glass to one side and inhaled the crisp night air. Winter in Florida held an appeal for Jack. With temperatures in the sixties during the day, he could participate in any number of outside sports. And when the night temps ran into the forties, it was cold enough for snuggling without frostbite.

Not that he had anyone to snuggle up to.

He hadn't met anyone he wanted to spend time with. When he'd worked as a PI, he'd seen enough cheating couples to know he wasn't in a hurry to jump into a relationship. After his last PI case, he stayed clear of romantic entanglements, including the idea of serious dating.

As his thoughts turned in that direction, he remembered the expression on Teri's face when he suggested they stay here tonight. Alone.

He chuckled as he gazed out into the night. He really had two reasons for her being here tonight. For one, he did want her help in discovering the phantom noises. And this was also a good way to gather more information on her for his reports to Kramer.

After all, Kramer had been in charge of the Daytona property where Teri worked before her transfer here. That transfer had raised questions in Jack's mind, and he'd wanted answers. Kramer supplied those answers. In return, Jack would keep an eye on Teri.

From the first day he arrived, Jack couldn't help but take notice of her. She knew her job, he had to give her that. He might even be interested in her if she wasn't so stiff and driven by her career. Yet her looks attracted him. Her wavy, toffee-hued hair curved around a face that held intelligent emerald eyes in a milk-and-roses complexion. She stood straight and tall, but fell short of his six foot frame. He only saw her in business suits, her 'armor' as he'd come to think of them. Teri seemed intent on all work and no play. He never saw her beyond the walls of the resort, and wondered if she'd ever been invited to off-hour gatherings.

A sharp rap on the door announced her arrival and the end of his reverie. He crossed the room and jerked open the door. A smile spread across his face. Instead of the armor, Teri wore jeans, a green sweatshirt and sneakers. She'd pulled her hair into a loose ponytail instead of that scalp-tugging bun. Another nice change.

"Great minds think alike," he said in greeting as his eyes glanced at her outfit.

Her eyebrows raised when her gaze traveled over their matching clothes. "Let's get to work," she said, brushing against him as she entered the room. One brief touch mixed with the subtle scent of her floral perfume as she breezed by, and Jack knew it was going to be a long night.

"So much for small talk," he drawled, amused by her all-work attitude.

She whirled around, hands on her hips. Her cheeks brightened in a becoming blush. "I'm here to get to the bottom of this problem, not play games, Jack."

"Who said anything about games?" Great, he had to spend the night with a spoilsport. "Look, I'm good at what I do. And I take *that* seriously."

He knew he sounded terse. Since turning thirty last month, he'd taken stock of his life and come to terms with his take-charge, get-the-job-done attitude. Long years of hard work for the corporation, and then his own firm, had steeled him.

"I'm sorry." She jammed her hands into her back pockets. "Sometimes I forget that not everyone works long hours like I do."

He took a deep breath, deciding to cut her some slack. "Look, I know we've rubbed each other the wrong way since I arrived. Let's use this time tonight as a way to get to know each other, as well as find the source of these noises."

She seemed to consider his words and, much to his surprise, she smiled. Her eyes lit up and the pinched, worried look disappeared, revealing a deceptively pretty face.

"What idea have you come up with?" she asked, albeit grudgingly. He realized how tough it was for her to give up the reins of control, especially if she felt her job was in jeopardy. But his reputation was at stake too, and he would do whatever necessary to keep things safe.

He motioned to the plans on the desk. "I thought it might help if we get an idea of the buildings' peculiarities."

"Have you found anything?" Her tone changed to business again.

He pointed to room 213. "According to the drawing, this wing was the first out-structure built. Below us are empty rooms identical to the one we're standing in, although some are being used to store construction materials left by the subcontractor. You can only get here by the outside walkway that connects this wing to the main building. All other exits are blocked until the work is completed."

"Hmm . . . it's odd that the subs never finished the job. I've wondered why someone would close off a perfectly suitable first floor, hire a contractor who deserts his job, then not pester him until the work is completed. Of course, now we know there are no permits." She tapped her finger against her chin. "But still, no one from corporate has instructed me on what to do next."

"I asked that same question when I started working here, but got a firm brush-off." He turned to face her. "Maybe you can do some digging on your own."

Teri looked up at him, her eyes wide and serious. "I have a friend who can find that type of information. I'll give her a call." She frowned. "I remember when we walked through that wing. Other than it being run down, the rooms are functional. Maybe there are structural defects?"

"I've checked out the area myself, numerous times. Everything seems in order, that's why the phantom noises bother me. If there was something drastically wrong, we'd have found it." He glanced down at the plans. "Obviously we don't see the problem. And there are no notes on these blueprints. We'll probably have to go down to the building department again or check with the zoning office for records of permits for any upgrades made throughout the years."

"Sounds like a reasonable next step. I can get Tom on it." Her voice lightened. "So, what do you propose we do while we wait for the ghost?"

Caught off-guard by her suggestion, he snapped his head up. Teri stood mere inches away, her arms folded over her chest, waiting for his response. In her relaxed stance, she invited a man's attentions. And she had his. Fully.

Wispy curls escaped the barrette, framing her delicate face. The subdued lighting of the room cast a soft glow over her features, catching a mischievous smile shimmering on her moist lips. He concentrated on swallowing before he did something stupid like reaching out to run his fingers over her satin skin.

"Well?" Impatience glittered in her intense green eyes and grated in her tone.

Rubbing his hand over his chin, Jack strode to the window, breathing in cool air. Tonight he found himself noticing her more than ever. Less as a colleague and more as a woman. If she continued to get to him like this, he'd either have to leave the room or kiss her. Either way, he'd be in trouble. Big trouble.

"I thought you might not have taken into consideration that we may be here all night, so I brought a deck of cards."

He threw a glance over his shoulder in time to see her extract a box of cards from her back pocket. It appeared she came prepared to spend a long night alone with him.

His mind ran through a list of games he would enjoy playing with her, but what would she propose? Go fish? Gin rummy? So tame, just like her. He let out a loud laugh.

"What's so funny?"

He turned to face her, the confusion shadowing her lovely face making him laugh more. "You don't want to know."

"Listen, Jack Bishop, I don't take very kindly to being the brunt of someone's joke, especially if I'm the punch line." She glared at him. "Are you going to tell me what you're thinking?"

He held up his hand. "That cards are just fine. Don't get uptight on me."

"Me? Uptight?"

"Yeah, you." His eyes bore into hers. "You are one of the most no-nonsense people I know."

"I am not."

He held back a chuckle. "Okay, then let's prove it." His mind raced for a game that would prove his point. "How about a variation on poker without betting money?"

Her eyes slitted. "What kind of variation?"

He walked over to the table and held a chair out for her. "Sort of like truth or dare," he improvised. "Whoever wins a hand gets to ask a personal question, or suggest something like a back rub, shoulder massage, that kind of thing." He tried to hold back a grin, sure she'd never go for his crazy idea.

"Let me get this straight," she said, opening the box of cards as she crossed the room. "Whoever wins a hand gets to make the demands? As long as it's within reason?"

"Of course," he answered innocently, already deciding to change the rules to his benefit as they went along.

She plopped down in a chair and shuffled the deck. "Okay. I'll deal the first hand. Five card stud, jokers wild."

His feeling of euphoria dropped a notch. "Sounds good."

Teri dealt the cards, her slender fingers deftly sending the cards sliding to his side of the table. She set the deck down and palmed the cards, her expression hidden behind shuttered eyes.

Oh great, a poker face. Jack leaned back, arranging the cards in his hand.

"I'll take three," he said, throwing the discards face down.

Teri gazed at him. "I'm set."

He frowned, glancing at his two jacks. Should he hold on or play again? "Two."

She dealt two more cards and he breathed a silent sigh when he picked up another jack. "Okay, let's see what you've got."

She placed her cards down in a flourish. Three queens.

Jack groaned.

"Now, let me get this straight. I get to ask you a question?" she asked sweetly.

He got the feeling he'd been had. "Or let me give you a shoulder rub?"

She shook her head, a smile playing on her lips. "I'll stick with a question." She looked at the ceiling, probably praying for inspiration, he thought.

"Oh, I've got one." She scooted up in her chair and rested her elbows on the table, her eyes locked on his.

"What is your secret for getting all my female employees to swoon at your feet?"

"Swoon?" Jack felt his face burn.

"Sure. Haven't you noticed the way they come around your office or just happen to run into you in the hallway?"

Did he notice? Jack rubbed his fingers over his forehead. He was nice to everyone, but no woman in particular. "That's nuts."

Teri gathered up the cards. "You really don't realize the effect you have on women?"

Jack grabbed them from her. "I don't have an effect and it's my turn to deal."

She held up her hands and smiled. "Okay, okay. Don't get so testy."

Easy for her to say. This wasn't how the game was supposed to go. He shuffled, called out the game, and dealt. When he picked up his cards, he nearly swore out loud.

"I'll take one," Teri said, her eyes leveled on her hand.

"I need two," he muttered, then brightened when he saw his draw. Two fours and three fives. *Hah,* he thought. *Beat that.* "Okay, let's see."

Jack laid down his cards, impatient to compare, only to stare incredulously at her winning hand. "A full house! You're a card shark."

She shrugged. "This was your idea."

Some idea. "What do you want this time?"

She pulled her leg up, anchoring her foot on the

chair and resting one arm over her bent knee. "What's your favorite color?"

As he reached to collect the cards, his hand stopped in mid-air. "That's all? No embarrassing questions?"

"Hey, I'm a nice girl."

Don't I know it. "Black." *Like my mood,* he grouched. He pushed the scattered cards into a pile. "Where'd you learn to play?"

Smiling, she held out her hand for the deck. "If you want a question answered, you'll have to win a hand."

They decided on another game and Teri dealt. After they both discarded and drew new cards, Jack called for them to show what they had.

"I won," he whooped, finally vindicated.

Teri chuckled and shook her head. "Aren't you the competitive one."

He grinned at her. "Maybe so, but now I get to pick." Crossing his arms over his chest, he lounged back in the chair. "Where'd you learn to play so well?"

She pursed her lips together, her eyes twinkling. "My dad taught me the basics, but I perfected my style in college."

"I figured you'd be the type to study all the time."

"I guess you thought wrong."

Jack gathered the cards again and they played another round, with Jack victorious once again. "For this part of the prize, I say we change the position of play and I get to make a request."

"Wait a minute," she cried, jumping up from her chair. "You can't make up the rules whenever you like."

"Didn't I tell you that after four games the winner gets to make a change?" He dragged his chair around the table to settle beside her. "Makes the game more challenging."

She lifted a dubious brow and planted her hands on her hips. "You failed to mention that little technicality."

He reclined in the chair. "When you win, you can change the rules."

She slowly returned to her seat. "If I didn't know better, I'd say these cards were marked."

Jack brushed the cards across the table and smoothly eased himself closer to her. He grinned when she didn't argue the maneuver. "Don't be a poor sport."

She glared at him. "Well, now what do you want?"

"A peck on the cheek."

Her eyes widened in horror. "What?"

"Come on." He pointed to his cheek as if she needed direction. "It's a simple request. A chaste kiss that will last no more than a second."

Her face turned an appealing shade of pink. He really expected her to chicken out. He'd only meant to tease her. Leaning close, he placed his hand on her knee for balance. She touched her lips to his face.

When she pulled away, their stares locked. For tense seconds neither one moved or breathed. The air filled with a static excitement. Mesmerized, Jack lowered his mouth, ready to cover hers, until he heard *tap . . . tap . . . tap.*

Chapter Four

"Did you hear that?" Teri whispered.

Jack had already bounded to his feet, zeroing in on the vicinity of the sound. He waved his hand at her. "Shh."

Stunned, Teri sat glued to the spot. There really were noises coming from this room. From her hotel. But how?

In the silence that followed, Teri held her breath. She strained to hear something more, anything, but only quiet echoed throughout the room.

She watched Jack cross the plush carpet and kneel at the foot of the bed. He tilted his head, a serious glint in his eyes. Finally. A glimpse of Jack in action.

Another faint tapping started up again, making her heart thud harder. Or was it because Jack had almost kissed her? She shook off that alarming thought and focused on Jack as he quickly crawled to the closet and opened the louvered door. He stuck his head inside and Teri could see his broad back, stone still as he listened.

Unable to contain her curiosity, she slid from the chair and tiptoed to Jack's side. She leaned toward the opening. Again, silence greeted her, so she bent over him, craning her neck to peer over his shoulder. The cramped space, filled only with shadows, gave her a chill. She tried to step back, and in doing so lost her balance and fell flat onto his back. The impact hit her like a lightning bolt. In a panic, she shoved herself off his broad shoulders, the force propelling him into the wall. She jerked upright, but not before banging into the wooden door.

He quickly turned and reached out to steady her, his fingers sending shivers up and down her arms. Just as quickly as he caught her, he let go, but the charged sensation still lingered.

Teri crossed her arms over her chest, trying to calm her erratic breathing. Stunned by her heated response to the accidental touch of Jack's body against hers, she struggled to conceal her distraught emotions.

"You okay?"

No, she thought. Tonight she almost let him kiss her. Kiss her! Yet she wanted him to . . . desperately.

To appease Jack's questioning stare, she nodded.

She hadn't reacted to a man this way in . . . well . . . never. Since she'd known Jack for such a short time, this didn't make sense. Did it? When he backed out of the closet she quickly jumped out of his way, afraid to make physical contact with him again.

He sighed, standing tall beside her. Dwarfed by this virile, rugged man, she rubbed her arms and dashed to the far side of the room.

"What now?" she asked in a subdued tone.

"It's so faint, I couldn't get a handle on it. The tapping has stopped for now, but we should hang around. Since we can't get into the adjoining rooms, we're stuck here." Crossing the room, he dragged one of the chairs to a spot beside the closet door. "We can take shifts if you want. It'll make it easier to get through the night."

"And you know this because you own a security firm?" She hated the sarcasm in her voice, but her heated reaction to him threw her off guard. And she couldn't let on that he affected her so . . . completely. "Have you been on a stake out before?"

"As a matter of fact, I have." He angled the chair partially into the empty closet. "I used to be a private detective. We learned this in, 'How to be a PI, 101.' "

She winced at his turn at sarcasm, deserving of his brusqueness. Still, it disturbed her when he returned her taunting remarks. The spark that flared between them earlier left her confused.

Looking over at him, she saw the tight, angry lines around his mouth. Awkwardly, she cleared her throat. "Do you think it will happen again?" Secretly, she hoped not. Right now she wanted the security of her own bed, huddled under her own blankets, alone with her whirlwind thoughts.

Jack shrugged, then grabbed a handful of the flowered coverlet and tugged it off the bed. "Who knows? We'd better stay, just in case."

Teri took the bedspread from him. "I'll take the first shift. I don't think I can sleep anyway."

"Okay. Wake me in a few hours." As if he didn't have a care in the world, Jack retreated to the bed, pulled off his shirt and threw it to a nearby chair. He drew back the covers, turned off the light and lay down. He moved about for a few seconds, then all motion ceased.

"Guys can sleep anywhere," she mumbled. She would never get comfortable tonight. In the sparse light of the half-moon, she located her tiny chair bed, then wrapped the spread around her, cocoon style. Having never had to sleep on one of the hotel chairs, she fussed and fumed about the lack of luxury for a hotel resort. If she wasn't already in management, she'd complain. Of course, if she were a guest, she wouldn't be in this uncomfortable position in the first place.

She stared across the room and out the window. The steady rhythm of Jack's breathing lured her into a semblance of calm. Unfortunately, it was a false sense of security.

Her stomach felt queasy when she thought about explaining this latest predicament to her superiors. They liked her, admired her management skills, but they still remembered the disappointing way she handled herself at the Daytona Beach Hotel.

Trying to lie on her side, Teri gathered the plush covers under her chin. The armrest dug into her side, the pain raw enough to compare with unpleasant times in Daytona.

It had been a nightmare instead of a dream come true. From the beginning, the hotel staff had been difficult to deal with, resenting the fact that the local manager hadn't been given the position of resident manager. Teri had worked hard for the job, working her way through Florida State by staying employed in her chosen field. She had years of experience, having been brought up by a father who worked as a live-in handyman for one hotel or another. She'd been exposed to every aspect of running a hotel, and it had been her father's wish that she earn her degree and be successful. To him, that meant a high-profile position in a four-star hotel. To her, it meant one day getting to Paris and having the prestige of working in a glamorous city.

The first doubts came in Daytona. Try as she might, she couldn't get any cooperation from the staff. That's when she'd adopted her tough boss persona. The tougher she became, the more her employees realized she meant business. Slowly, over the five years she worked there, her carefree personality had changed. As an exacting businesswoman, she'd earned the respect of her fellow workers, but at the expense of forgetting the real Teri. The fun-loving woman slipped away, to be replaced by the woman she was now. Cold. Unrelenting.

Jack rolled over, his sudden motion startling Teri from her thoughts. He'd heard about her troubles. Even had the gall to mention it to her.

In retrospect, she realized that her new personality kept her from being more tolerant of people's needs. When the controller's personal problems overstepped work boundaries, she should have tried to help him deal with his problems instead of brushing him off. By then, the bookkeeping didn't add up. If she'd been more of a friend, he might not have resorted to embezzling from the corporation.

Teri had quickly straightened out the mess. When she finally told her boss, Mr. Kramer, he read her the riot act, but he didn't do anything about the problem. Two weeks later she received a written reprimand and a transfer.

With a huff, Teri threw off the spread, too agitated to lie still. She walked to the window, gazing out into the lonely bleak darkness. When had her life started to take on the characteristics of the night? Void. Colorless. Solitary.

She rubbed her hands over her arms. The warm fleece of the sweatshirt fought off the chill invading her limbs. The hope that coming to Clearwater Beach would change things stayed foremost in her mind. She had a second chance. She planned to use it well.

"A penny for your thoughts."

Teri jumped, startled by the quiet words spoken in the dead of the night and reaching into her most private domain.

"Geez, Jack, you scared me." Her eyes narrowed as she tried to focus on him in the darkness. "How long have you been awake?"

A pale shaft of moonlight fell over him as he pushed

away the sheet, pulling himself forward to sit on the edge of the bed. He yawned loudly while stretching his arms high over his head.

"Long enough to watch you stare out the window. Such a pensive expression for an attractive woman."

Teri felt herself blush at his compliment, grateful for the shadows hiding her telltale reaction.

"Are you going to tell me what's going on in that head of yours? Or should I guess?"

"Go ahead and try. You already know everything else about me."

"I'll bet you were thinking about your future at West Wind."

She wanted to argue with him, wanted to tell him his observations were way off base. She really wanted to, but he was right. With a nod, she slid down onto the windowsill.

The intimacy of the quiet room and the dim shadows lent an air of camaraderie. Secrets could be revealed here, in the depths of the night. She needed a friend. And Jack was the only one available right now.

"Something like that. Instead of dwelling on current problems, I've been wallowing in my past defeat."

"Been there. Not a great way to move forward."

Taking a deep breath, she ran her palms over denim jeans and continued. "Do you ever wonder if a person can learn from his mistakes?"

"Or her mistakes?" he asked gently.

She sighed deeply, pushing back strands of hair that had escaped her ponytail. "That too."

Jack rose from the bed and in two steps stood beside

her, a mere breath away. Now it was his turn to regard the black sky, to seek answers from the night while she waited patiently for his words. She glanced at his powerful chest and suddenly wished he would wrap his arms around her and pull her into his strength, offering her comfort.

He turned his head slowly, his intelligent eyes full of understanding. "You want to know if you should take the conservative route, inform the corporate bigwigs before disaster strikes. Then again, nothing could come of this, and you'll look incompetent, like you can't handle internal problems."

"Exactly," she whispered. "What should I do?"

"Just what you're doing."

Teri entered her office the next morning just as the phone buzzed. "Corporate headquarters on line one, Miss Price."

"I'll take it in my office."

She took a deep breath, and smoothed her ivory linen suit before clasping the receiver. "Teri Price."

"Teri, it's Don Kramer. How are you?"

"Fine, Don." No point in beating around the bush. "How can I help you?"

"I'm scheduling a visit to Florida. I'll be down the weekend after next. That should give you plenty of time to prepare for your review."

Two weeks? "Everyone here will look forward to your visit."

"Excellent. Until then."

Teri replaced the handpiece with a trembling hand.

Of all people, why did Don Kramer have to be the general manager? He'd been the one in charge of cleaning up the Daytona fiasco and recommended she be transferred to West Wind.

"He must have disaster radar," she mumbled under her breath.

A knock on the door startled her. Her assistant, Tom, opened it and stuck his head in. "Mr. Bishop would like to see you as soon as you have a free moment."

Teri sighed. "Tell him I'll meet him shortly."

She wasn't ready to see Jack just now. Not so soon after her conversation with Kramer. Stretching, she kicked off her pumps and curled her toes into the plush moss green carpet. With a shake of her head, she sat down at her the oak desk and flipped through her paperwork.

After ten minutes of trying to concentrate, her mind refused to focus on the task. She tossed the papers on the blotter, then leaned back into the comfort of her leather chair. Resting her chin on steepled fingers, she scrutinized her office. The professional elegance made her feel at home, and the ivy plants and a few pictures added a personal touch. Across the room on a polished credenza sat a collection of glazed pottery, her one interest outside work. She sighed, wishing she had time to take classes and create art herself. That, along with a long list of desires, would have to wait.

She turned her attention back to the demands at hand when suddenly, unbidden, the vision of Jack in the shadows last night sprang into her mind. She recalled his reassuring voice when he offered her advice. The ten thousand dollar question loomed before her: should she trust a man who had a stake in this? Why had he suddenly taken an interest in her welfare? What was in it for him?

That's three questions, she told herself. But still she had no answers. She wanted to trust Jack. His inner strength appealed to her. Solid, a man to help in a disaster. And the current situation qualified as such.

Add that to the fact that she found him incredibly attractive, and that meant trouble. The way she responded to his look, his touch, was completely out of her realm of experience. Her dates with men were few and far between. She'd never experienced the personal dilemma of being attracted to someone she had to work with before. It left her feeling out of control, and she refused to allow this circumstance to rattle her.

She rose from the chair and found her shoes, ignoring the papers scattered across her desk. "Later," she announced to the empty room, then headed out the door in search of Jack.

Within minutes she found him. She stared inside his office, feeling guilty. Granted, it was a makeshift office, but her office was spacious and lavishly decorated. Jack's space consisted of an old metal desk, a few card table chairs, and a filing cabinet.

Her gaze traveled to his desk, where she spied him working on a state-of-the-art computer system, with a fax, modem, video equipment and other electronic doodads she didn't recognize. In this arena, Jack's system was far superior to her own.

"Is he busy?" Teri whispered to Ed Raven. She always thought his name apropos, with his dark slicked-back hair, beady eyes behind thick glasses, and beaky nose.

Ed nodded. "He's just answering an e-mail. Have a seat."

Teri sidled her way around the desk, tugging her linen skirt as she lowered herself onto one of the folding chairs. Her eyes scanned the room, stopping with interest at the sports memorabilia. She looked at Jack, only to find him staring directly at her, his eyes gleaming with interest.

He hit a key and smiled. "Well, Miss Price, now you see how the other half lives."

"That's quite a set-up you have. Do you use all that equipment?"

"Sure do. These days you have to keep on top of everything. I can get on the Internet and find out anything I need to know about the latest in hotel security." His eyes flashed wickedly as his fingers pecked over the keyboard, typing in commands. "Want me to see what I can dig up on you?"

She waved her hand. "No, thanks. Just ask me what you want to know. And let's skip the deck of cards."

"I just might take you up on that." His gaze met hers and she felt that tug of excitement deep within her. She couldn't break the connection, couldn't blink if her life depended on it. So she didn't try, until Ed cleared his throat.

"Excuse me, Jack. I've got rounds. So, if you need to talk to me . . ."

"No, go on. I'll catch you later," Jack replied, his voice composed while his eyes, still aimed at her face, held an enigmatic gaze.

The room fell silent, but Teri felt her heart hammering to the beat of calypso drums. Embarrassed, she looked away. "Let's get back to business."

Jack grinned, but took her cue. "Even though we didn't hear anything after those first few tapping sounds last night, something *is* wrong and we need to find out what it is."

"I have a suggestion," Teri offered.

"Let's hear it."

"Martin Pressman, from the historical society, seems to know a great deal about the hotel. He told me his father worked here when the wings were being constructed. He might be able to help us."

"Do you trust him enough to involve him?"

"Yes, I do. He has knowledge of West Wind that we'll never find on our own. Even your computer won't have that kind of personal information." She had to convince Jack, because deep down she knew Martin could help.

Jack rested his elbows on the desk and dropped his chin on folded hands, intently focusing on her.

Teri squirmed under his perusal. If she caved now, she sensed that Jack would never take her seriously.

"Okay, we'll give Pressman a chance."

Teri expelled the breath she was holding. "Great. What else do you think we should do?"

"We should search the wing again. This time with

a more discerning eye. We need to find something out of the ordinary."

Shifting in her seat, Teri couldn't ignore the sinking sensation in her stomach. "You really think there's something strange going on here, don't you?"

"I think we should consider the worst case scenario and act accordingly. Always be prepared, that's my motto."

"That's the Boy Scout motto."

He scratched his head. "Really? I knew I heard it somewhere."

"Okay. We'll talk to Martin tomorrow."

"Now. We're going now. Together."

"Jack, I have to work."

He stood, hitting a few more buttons on the keyboard. Then he walked to her, his hands grazing her neck before settling on her shoulders. "This is work. We are a team, remember? Two people gathering information are always better than one."

Her mind went blank when he touched her. His touch warmed not only her shoulders but radiated over her entire body.

"Go grab your purse, tell Tom to take over, call Martin, and let's get out of here. It's a great day, why don't you try to enjoy it."

She gave a fake huff and headed for the door. "If you weren't so pushy, maybe I would."

"That's the spirit." He stood back and regarded her. "You know, you're really very pretty when you relax. Try doing it more often."

She stood rooted to the spot. Jack's eyes smoldered

and he tilted his head toward her. She thought he was going to kiss her, but he placed his hand on the small of her back to escort her from the room. Relief and disappointment surged through her.

Chapter Five

"Look, I know you don't like being off the property, but nothing earth shattering is going to happen in an hour or two," Jack said as he drove down the main street. "If anything, you might pick up some interesting tidbits to tell the guests. You could start a bulletin board with local stories and gossip. Tourists love that stuff."

Since they'd left the hotel, Jack had tried to relieve Teri's anxiety about leaving the property. He really meant it when he said they were in this together.

"You're just trying to appeal to my business sense." Rubbing her finger against her chin, Teri smiled. "And it's working. Actually, that bulletin board is a great idea."

On the short ride to the north end of the beach, Teri threw out ideas for a marketing ploy involving local history. He had to admit, she was good at her job. For

50

what seemed like the hundredth time, he wondered why Kramer had it out for her.

After a few minutes, she rolled down her window, a cool breeze carrying her words away. Jack made a few turns and suddenly the main road came to an abrupt end. A weather-beaten street sign hung at a crooked angle on a long pole. The natural elements had worn off the lettering, but Jack could make out the wording: Pressman Estates.

"This is the place?" Teri asked, adjusting her sunglasses as she read the letters.

Jack shrugged. "Must be. Let me see your directions again."

She handed him a piece of hotel stationary with Martin's directions printed neatly in Teri's handwriting. "It says here to follow the driveway until we reach his place."

"You call this a driveway?" Teri asked, pointing to the narrow road consisting of murky sand, broken shells and pot holes. In the distance, Jack could make out the shape of a structure, presumably Pressman's house.

"Well, are you going?"

Jack counted to ten. Miss Bossy giving the orders as usual.

He stepped on the gas pedal, expertly leading his truck over the bumpy road. Shells crunched beneath the tires. The unmistakable scent of surf and sand invaded the cab. "Guess Pressman doesn't use the drive much."

A cottage stood nestled within lush vegetation. Teri

audibly drew in her breath. "It's beautiful," she whispered.

Jack, for once, agreed.

Designed in the fashion of an old Florida cracker house, a wide porch wrapped around the entire one-story dwelling, inviting the weary traveler to rest a while. Gingerbread lattice curved into the porch corners. Pristine white shutters graced windows set in a yellow house warmed by the late morning sun.

Rocking chairs, angled in groups on the porch, swayed gently in the wind. Jack noticed a stained glass etching in the front door just before it opened and Martin stepped out.

Jack jumped out of the truck, then walked around to help Teri down. When she saw Martin on the porch, she quickly approached him.

"What a wonderful place you have!"

"Thank you." Martin held out his hand in greeting. "How are you, Mr. Bishop?"

"Call me Jack." He clasped the older man's hand, surprised by the strength there.

"Come inside," Martin beckoned. After a brief tour of the house, he led them onto the back porch.

The end of the backyard lay five hundred yards from where they stood, with the beach spread out before them. Sea grass grew in profusion and seagulls dipped in and out of the water, squawking as they made lazy circles.

A light breeze ruffled Teri's thick hair, pulling strands loose from her severe hairstyle. Jack did a double take. The sun brightened her soft tresses, her cheeks were flushed with excitement and her eyes twinkled, full of delight. Here in the full light of day, she was quite stunning.

"Jack? Did you hear me?"

He swallowed, appalled that his mind turned traitor on him. "What?" he asked, trying to pick up a thread of the conversation.

"I said, isn't it lovely here?"

He nodded. "Incredible."

Teri tilted her head, regarding him with questions in her eyes.

Get a grip, Bishop. He stared at her until an amused voice summoned his attention.

"Sit," Martin instructed. They gathered around a table laid out with cups, saucers, and a steaming pot beside a plate of pastries. "I took the liberty of making tea before you arrived."

Martin poured, then stared at Jack, intelligent eyes reflecting curiosity. "Miss Price has expressed an interest in the history of West Wind. She mentioned some problems?"

Jack nodded. "We're concerned about the Jacaranda wing."

Martin steepled his long, crooked fingers beneath his chin and leaned back into his patio chair. "And as fellow employees, you two are searching for answers?"

Teri gazed into her teacup while Jack cleared his throat. "Both of us care only about the best interests of the hotel."

Martin grinned, his gaze moving back and forth over his guests faces. "The hotel's best interests?"

"Yes," Teri replied in a subdued tone.

The old man smiled, his eyes alive in the weathered face. Strands of gray hair danced in the wind. "I know a great deal about this island. I've lived here my entire life. Mostly, I know the history. I know the rumors from truth. And you know, truth is sometimes stranger than fiction."

Teri leaned forward, resting her elbows on the table. "You mean about West Wind?"

Martin raised his cup for a drink, hands slightly trembling as he replaced it on the saucer. "Ah, now there's a story."

Jack glanced at Teri. She scooted to the end of her seat, obviously enthralled by this man. Would she ever look at him with that much interest? Then he wondered why it should matter.

Unexpectedly, she returned his gaze, her look almost victorious, like she had one up on him. Their gazes locked, and for a moment he could have sworn she softened before abruptly turning away. When Martin spoke again, he reluctantly focused his attention back to the conversation.

"The hotel was one of the first commercial structures built on the beach. Its grand design and elegant furnishings brought in an exclusive clientele, people rich enough to afford the exorbitant prices, even back then.

"As the resort grew more popular, so did the demand for more rooms. My father worked on the construction of the three wings and later tended to the grounds. A playground for the wealthy, he called it. Many famous movie stars, bankers, railroad tycoons, even gangsters came here for the sun and tranquility."

"Gangsters?" Teri laughed. "Like who?"

"Al Capone for one."

"Get out! *The* Al Capone?" Her tone held distinct skepticism.

Martin chuckled. "Yes, indeed. He wasn't a stranger to the Gulf coast."

"This is amazing," Teri said, swiveling in her seat. "I never thought we'd learn anything like this, did you, Jack?"

Jack shook his head, drawn into the story despite himself.

"There's a lot of rumor mixed with truth, as with most hotel gossip, but the story gets better. In the late 1920's, Capone came down to visit, supposedly to check on his investments. Actually, there was trouble in Chicago and he had to leave town in a hurry.

"He stayed at West Wind for a few months, an extended visit. Some of his associates stayed with him. Mostly likely they were his bodyguards."

Jack looked out over the endless blue water, his mind mulling over this information. "Was there ever any trouble?"

Martin folded his hands over his stomach. "Just before Capone left, there was a robbery at a jewelry store on the mainland. Although he was never officially accused of the crime, the coincidence was too obvious."

"Why?" Teri piped in.

"You see," Martin explained, "Capone bragged about the beautiful jewels he got for his wife, what a deal they were. He planned to surprise her when he got home."

Jack rubbed his chin. "But that doesn't prove he *stole* them. The guy was rich, why would he bother with a robbery in a small town? He had enough trouble waiting for him back home."

Martin shrugged. "Like I said, rumor mixed with truth. The bottom line is, the jewels were never recovered."

Teri's eyes widened. "Never recovered?"

"Not to my knowledge. I was a young boy when I heard the stories. All I know was that he left the hotel, never to return."

"Were there ever any problems with remodeling?" Jack asked, bringing the topic back to the reason they came here in the first place.

"My father told me a few years later, one wing in particular had rather odd happenings within its walls. Strange noises that scared the guests. But that was a long time ago."

"Was anything done about it?" Teri asked.

"I'm afraid the stories were just tales, perhaps created to lend an air of mystery to an already popular resort. Nothing was ever discovered to give credence to the claims."

The telephone rang inside the house. Martin excused himself.

"Jack, I'm so glad you talked me into coming here. What an unbelievable story."

"Maybe not. I grew up not far from here and I remember hearing rumors about Capone. But I never knew if the gossip was true."

"There must be more to those stories about the strange noises than Martin knows. You think the contractor disappeared because he was spooked?"

"No. There are plenty of other companies that could have come in and bid for the job. Not everyone believes in ghosts."

She rolled her eyes. "We're back to that again?"

"I don't know." Feeling more frustrated than when the search began, he stood, massaging the taut muscles in his neck. Squinting his eyes, he peered out over the crystal water.

He sensed her eyes on him and turned slowly to look at Teri. A smile tugged at her lips, shy at first, and her gaze pinned his. They stared at each other for a tense minute until she slowly rose from her seat and walked to the porch railing.

"Care to talk a stroll to the point?"

He hesitated. Did he want to be alone with her? Walking on the beach always conjured romantic images in his mind, and he didn't want to start down that road. "What about Martin?"

"It's not far. I don't think he'll mind. Besides, you're the one who said I should relax more. Now is a perfect opportunity."

He had said so, really just to irritate her. But now, using his own words against him, she cast out her hook to snag him. When she started down the steps, he followed, taking the bait.

*   *   *

Teri couldn't believe her impromptu offer. Maybe the story she'd just heard made her feel reckless. Maybe it was the glorious clear day, spent with a man she couldn't fight her attraction to any longer. Maybe the salt air went right to her head.

For the first time in a long time, she was glad to be away from work and all its pressures. When she saw Jack's eyes darken as he stood beside her, she wanted this moment to last forever.

Slipping off her pumps, she hopped off the bottom step that led to the beach. Warm sand filtered through her hose. She wiggled her toes, enjoying the small sense of freedom. Jack removed his shoes and socks and they were off, strolling along the water.

The crisp salty air was invigorating. Impulsively, she reached up to shake her hair from its combs, revelling in the sensation as it caressed her neck and swirled around her shoulders.

On impulse she quickly removed her stockings. "No point in ruining my hose," she commented, keeping her voice light and playful. She stuffed the bunched nylons into her purse, then peeked under her lashes at Jack, taking delight in his shocked expression. So much for him thinking she couldn't relax. After this, Jack would never know what to expect from her. She liked that idea.

As they neared the point, the sand grew more coarse and the surf hit the beach with a heavy pounding. Jack grabbed hold of her arm, pulling her to a safe distance from the frothing surf. "The undertow here is strong.

When the water meets at the point, the tides can be dangerous."

She nodded. The warm sunlight kissed her cheeks as she raised her face like a flower opening to the rays. She closed her eyes against the glare, feeling more alive in this moment than she had in years.

"A day at the beach will never be the same," Jack said in a husky whisper. He squeezed her arm, but made no other moves toward her.

Teri opened her eyes and smiled at him. She purred in contentment. Here she stood, on a beautiful beach, beside a gorgeous man who set her heart afire. At this moment, she could almost forget his interference in her career.

His head lowered toward her for what she felt sure would be a mind-boggling kiss. The clean scent of his cologne tickled her nose as he drew closer. His lips barely grazed hers. In anticipation of more, she waited, holding her breath. A ringing sounded in her ears.

How romantic, she thought, *I'm hearing bells.* The ringing sounded again, this time with an urgent tone. She looked up at Jack.

"Your cellular," he muttered, dropping his hand and taking a step back.

"Of course. My phone," she replied briskly, pulling the shoulder strap of her purse down to reach inside the leather bag. "Hello?"

"Miss Price, it's Tom. We have a problem with one of the guests. I tried to find Jack so he could handle it, but he's off the property. The guest insists on speaking to the manager. I've stalled as long as I can, but I think you really should get back here."

She glanced at her watch, her business alter ego kicking in. "Tell them I'll be there in fifteen minutes."

A pause. "Miss Price, I can hardly hear you. What's all that noise I'm hearing?"

"Ummm . . . seagulls. I'm driving by the beach," she fibbed. "I'm on my way back, so you'll have to handle things for a few more minutes." She pressed the end button, annoyed with herself for abandoning her work, but even more annoyed with Jack. Why did the staff always call Jack before her? *She* was in charge.

"I've got to get back." She shot him an accusatory glance. "I knew this was a bad idea. I should have stayed put."

Jack's expression turned perplexed. When he stepped back, she saw as much as felt him withdraw to the offensive, and she knew they'd reverted back to square one.

"Yeah, well, Martin is your friend. Sorry you think leaving the hotel to get some answers was a bad idea. Hope Martin and I didn't ruin your day." He turned on his heel, stalking back to the house.

She jogged behind him, fuming now that he turned this on her. She was the one who deserved to be angry. All the salt air and Jack's riveting male presence had made her lose sight of her goal.

Martin had returned to his chair by the time they got back from the beach. He rose to meet them as they brushed the sand from their feet before slipping on their shoes. "Is something wrong? You both seemed to enjoy your stroll but now you're frowning."

"No, I'm not," they answered in unison.

His eyebrows rose in surprise. "My mistake."

Teri stepped up and took his hand. "Please, Martin, forgive me. I received a call and we have to leave. We're actually here on company time."

"Then by all means, you should get back."

Jack shook Martin's hand. "Thanks for the history lesson."

"My pleasure. And remember, both of you are welcome here. I'll tell you more stories of the rich and famous guests that have stayed at your hotel."

Teri smiled. "I'd like that."

She walked to the truck in brisk steps, waving goodbye once she was settled in the cab. "Hurry," she said loud enough for Jack to hear.

"Hold your horses," he grumbled as he turned the ignition. "I'll have you back to your precious hotel quick enough."

She kept quiet during the drive, covertly sneaking peeks at Jack as he drove. His thumb beat a steady rhythm on the steering wheel. Her curt words hung in the air between them.

When Jack pulled into his parking space, Teri nearly jumped out of the cab before he came to a complete stop. She had one foot on the ground when Jack called her name.

She stepped out completely before turning around. "What is it?" she asked, her tone full of impatience.

Jack gazed at her, emotion hidden from the brown

depths of his eyes. "Don't you think you should put your stockings on before you head into the lobby?"

Appalled by her own forgetfulness, she looked down at her bare legs. What had she been thinking, playing on work time? Instead of taking his advice, she glared at him before turning on her heel and stomping off.

"By the way," he called after her, "When you're finished with your pressing emergency, come to my office. We have to make hunting plans."

She spun around, her face heated with frustration. "For what?"

"The stolen jewels Martin told us about. I have a gut suspicion that they're somewhere in our hotel."

Chapter Six

By the time Teri finally made it to Jack's office, the night shift had taken over. She poked her head into his office, finding it empty. Taking a quick look around, she ducked into the room and sat down. With a husky sigh, she removed her shoes and started to massage one foot. Pumps may make a fashion statement, but they were murder on the toes.

Replacing her shoes, Teri headed to the door, wanting to go in search of him, and collided right into him. She grabbed a handful of shirt to brace herself, crumpling the soft material beneath. A deep flush covered her face.

"What's your hurry?" he asked, clutching her upper arms to keep her firmly in place. She was afraid to move, afraid to let her heart hope that a relationship could happen between them. As much as she hated to admit it, he was slowly easing his way into her well-organized, no-nonsense life.

She swept a glance over his face, noting the sparkle of confidence and amusement lurking in his brown eyes. As effective as cold water, that look returned her sanity.

"I was looking for you," she replied, wiggling out of his grasp. She brushed her sleeves and skirt and put herself back in order. At least on the outside. In her mind she imagined herself as prey trapped in a web, waiting for the spider to attack. Only this predator was tall, strong, handsome, and infinitely more dangerous to her carefully planned life.

He leaned against the door jamb, crossing his arms in a deceptively lazy manner. But she noticed his frown. Evidently he, too, was affected by their encounter. She hoped he couldn't tell how deeply it rattled her.

"You found me. I'm touched that you felt the need to rush into my arms after our prolonged separation."

"You—what?" she sputtered, taken aback by the annoyance she heard in his statement.

Jack strode to his desk. "I asked a friend to check on that robbery Martin told us about. He looked into some old police records and found out that the jewels were extremely valuable. After almost sixty years, they could be worth a fortune, especially with the folklore attached to them."

"Any idea who stole them?"

He shook his head, handing her the paper so she

could read the message herself. "The police never had enough conclusive evidence to make an arrest."

Teri handed the fax back to Jack. "Earlier today you said the jewels might be here, in West Wind. Why do you think that?"

He lowered himself into his chair, dropping his feet onto the desk with a plop and nonchalantly crossing them at the ankles. As he spoke, he grabbed a pencil and balanced it between his fingers. "I can't prove anything, but it's a strong hunch. If Capone didn't steal the jewelry, then maybe one of his visiting buddies did. What a perfect place to hide an expensive heist—right here under the noses of the rich."

Teri considered the possibility. "It is a long shot."

Jack set his feet on the floor, then leaned his elbows on the desk. He pointed the eraser end of the pencil at her. "Okay, consider this. Suppose they bring the loot back here, intending to sneak it out when they left. Suddenly Capone hightails it back to Chicago. Maybe there was no time to retrieve the jewels and they remained here, locked away in their hiding place."

"But wouldn't someone come back for them? If they're worth that much, I know I'd get here somehow."

He shrugged and leaned back into the chair. "Maybe the thief died. You've heard the stories about all the gangland killings. If this guy was a pal of Capone's, he might have lived a short life."

Placing her hands on her hips, Teri frowned. "So what's the next step?"

"Two things." His expression grew pensive. "One, we should search the closed wing again. Those noises had to come from somewhere, even if we couldn't place them." He leaned toward her, whispering, "Remember, we don't want the guests complaining."

Teri groaned. "Please, don't remind me."

Chuckling, Jack stood and glanced at his watch. "It's almost nine o'clock. I can rustle up some flashlights if you want to poke around."

"And the second thing?"

"The historical society is giving a ball Friday night. I think we should attend and gather information. Martin will be there, so he can help too."

Stunned by his invitation she said, "You mean, like a date?"

"Yeah." He hesitated. "A date."

"Sounds like a plan." Teri's heart pounded at the prospect of acting on solid information. *Not so*, her mind whispered. *You want to go out with Jack. Away from the hotel.* "I've got some clothes in my office. Give me fifteen minutes to change and I'll meet you in the lobby."

Jack smiled. "That's my girl."

His girl. It should have made her bristle, but in truth, she liked the sound of it.

Jack flicked the light switch several times. Nothing happened. "That's strange. Last time I was down here the electricity worked."

"Maybe Capone's ghost returned to the scene of the crime and cut the wires."

"Great deduction, Madame Detective, but don't get too worked up until we find some evidence."

"Sorry, I was only going along with your theory. Now what?"

"Turn on the flashlight."

"Why, are you afraid of the dark?"

"Funny." He clicked on his light. "No, we'll check out a couple of rooms tonight, then come back during the day."

"Let's go in here," she suggested as they approached the first room.

Flashing his light into the interior of the room, Jack noticed that the layout was the same as every room in the hotel, but the decorating had been long neglected. Furniture cluttered the room.

"Look at all this stuff. What a waste leaving it here to collect dust." Teri walked over to a stack of bed frames placed against the wall, shining her light on them. "These frames are in excellent condition. If the hotel can't use them anymore, we could at least donate them to a local woman's charity or shelter."

"Good idea." He pointed the flashlight to the floor, searching for clues. Not seeing a thing, he moved the light along the walls, then up to the ceiling. Nothing out of the ordinary. He backed up, bumping into Teri. She jumped, as if branded by a red-hot poker.

"Sorry," she mumbled.

He flashed the light at her, her eyes wide. She quickly turned away. What had he done now?

Returning to the task at hand, he looked around some more, disappointed at their slow progress. Time to get Teri and move on. Turning the light on her, he caught her down on her knees before an outlet.

"What're you doing?"

She glanced back at him, her face half-hidden in the shadows. "I'm checking out anything that might be suspicious. Don't you watch mystery movies? Jewelry pieces are generally small and can be hidden in an unobtrusive spot, like a wall outlet."

"And how do you expect to see anything through the cover?"

With a single movement, she produced a screwdriver she'd carried with her and held it up for his inspection.

"Dad was a handyman. Taught me everything I know."

"I have to hand it to you. When you're right, you're right."

He dropped to his knees beside her, flashing the light into any area that might conceal smaller objects. Suddenly Teri jolted backwards and climbed his arm.

"What's wrong?"

"Bugs! Swarming out of the outlet. I hate bugs."

He stared down at her, perplexed. *This woman could probably handle hostile troops and she freaks out over bugs?* Had to be a woman thing.

After long minutes, Teri's breath slowed. She pushed away from him. "We have work to do."

He tried to hold back a grin. "Right. Let's get to it."

After a half hour of searching room after empty room, Jack sank down by a closet door. "I'm going to have to study the blueprints again before we come back. Most of the molding and outlets look pretty old. Not the original fixtures, but older than the rooms we use now."

Teri sat beside him. "We could also check to see if there were any changes made that would affect the closets and windows. You know, look for hiding places."

Jack laid his hand on her knee, feeling the warmth of her body emanate from beneath her jeans. As usual, she looked great when she lost the severe suits. She seemed more relaxed wearing a cropped gold sweater and letting her hair loose around her face so the waves rested on her shoulders. He caught a whiff of her floral scent. It was all he could do to keep from hauling her onto his lap.

"I'm really impressed at your skills of deduction. You missed your calling. You should have been a detective."

She shrugged. "Thanks, but I'm not interested." A pause. "You're not so bad yourself."

"Really? Some people's opinions would differ."

She shifted. "Like who?"

"My family, for one." Now he'd gone and done it—he'd opened his big mouth. What was it about her that caused him to let his guard down? He didn't discuss his family with anyone.

"You don't have a good relationship with them?"

He stretched out his long legs. As night descended, a breeze from the water whipped up. A chill invaded the room. He crossed his arms over his chest, his thick sweatshirt keeping him warm.

"No. I don't see them often, and I sure don't tell them much of what I do these days." He left it at that.

She reached out to graze his hand, a shy gesture that touched him deeply. She had an innocent air, yet at the same time, so alluring. "My father lived my career along with me until he passed away." Her voice grew soft. "That's why he urged me to get a good education. I think he would have loved my job."

"What did he do?"

"He worked for one hotel or another all my life. Grounds keeper, handyman, you name it. We lived on the properties where he worked, mostly small family-owned establishments."

He grinned. "So that's when you got hooked?"

Teri shook her head. "Not really hooked. When I was old enough, I worked too. I learned just about everything there is to know about running a hotel before I went to college."

"Let me guess," Jack deduced. "This was all your father's dream, not yours."

She sighed. "It's not that I didn't want a career. I just don't know if hotel management would have been my first choice. Dad was so excited, I couldn't let him down."

"And now?"

"Now I'm working on my promotion to Paris. The City of Lights."

Silence settled over the room while Jack pondered her words. How important was this promotion to her? And why did the thought of her leaving not sit right with him? He didn't want to go there, so he changed the subject. "What about your mom?"

"She died." Teri removed her hand from his. "When I was young."

"Sorry." So, she'd traveled around a lot as a kid. Maybe that explained why she was such a loner. Or maybe she was lonely?

He rubbed his hand over her leg, intending only to convey his sympathy. Teri tensed and jumped up as though the room were on fire and they had to make a fast escape. A jolt of frustration swept through him at her rebuff. He could have sworn she was beginning to relax in his company.

Clenching his fist, he decided not to push her. She'd come a long way since the first day he arrived and he didn't want to risk losing her as a partner. "Let's check room 113 again. If the strange noises originated in there, we might find something."

She nearly ran out the door before Jack had risen to his feet. If she was feeling the same as he, their nearness to one another would set them both off kilter.

"Are you coming?" he heard her yell from another room. Shaking his head, he pulled himself together before joining her.

"Any luck?" he asked, entering the room.

"It's pretty much the same as the last room, except for some construction material left behind by our elusive contractor." She held her flashlight directly ahead of her, then deadpanned, "Oh, and a really big hole in the wall."

Jack followed the beam of light with his eyes, astonished that anyone would leave a gaping hole such as this open. He approached slowly. "This wasn't here last time I checked the wing."

"When was that?"

"Last weekend."

Teri hovered close behind, as if hiding behind him in case something jumped out. "That explains the noises. Maybe someone's been searching for the jewels since then. Something made them stop and they left without closing the hole."

"Another detective theory?"

She clutched his arm. "Don't get sarcastic. It could happen."

"I think it's more likely someone was checking the electric."

"Yeah, with a really big hammer."

He moved closer, pointing. "See, some of the wires have been pulled loose. If it needs to be rewired, permits would have to be pulled."

"Back to square one again." Her shoulders slouched.

"Don't sound so disappointed." He aimed the light into the darkness of the inner wall.

"Maybe this is where our sounds came from. What if an animal crawled inside and couldn't get out?" He heard the doubt in her voice.

"That may be, but what about the noises Martin told us about? That was long before someone made this hole. And long before animals may or may not have taken up residency."

Jack scanned the room, wishing for better lighting.

"I hate to admit it, but I don't think we'll find much more. And we haven't heard any noises tonight. Let's say we call it quits until we can recruit some sunlight."

Teri flashed the light around the room one last time. "I agree. Maybe things will be clearer then."

"I don't know about that," Jack muttered under his breath. Every moment spent with Teri sent him into chaos, pleasurable though it might be.

"What did you say?" she asked, stepping toward him.

"Nothing. Forget it."

Her soft acceptance had him wondering if she'd heard him after all. Her sweet elusive expression got the best of him. He reached out, placing his hands around her arms to pull her into him. Wrapping her in an embrace sure to dazzle any woman, he waited for resistance, but received none. For a fraction of a second he hesitated before lowering his head to kiss her. After all, each time he touched her tonight she acted uncomfortable.

But he wanted this. With the decision made, his lips touched hers.

The jarring sound of a door slamming jolted Jack to reality. Teri jumped, disengaging herself from him. She brushed her fingers over her lips, gazing up at him. A hint of confusion marred her dazed expression.

"Hey, anybody in here?" called a male voice.

"Ed," Jack whispered on a harsh breath. Then he shouted, "We're in room 113."

Ed bumped into the wall before stumbling into the

room. "Man, it's dark in here. Don't you guys believe in lights?"

"They're out," Jack replied, never taking his eyes from Teri's pale face. "Guess we'll call the electrician tomorrow."

"Good idea," Ed muttered.

Teri cleared her throat. "If you men will excuse me, I need to get home."

She brushed past Jack. He made no move to stop her. He felt as shaken as she looked.

"Was it something I said?" Ed asked.

Jack sighed, scoring his hand through his hair. "No. We didn't find a thing. I think she's just tired."

"Good, 'cause I don't want her mad at me. I saw her get on Tom last week—it wasn't a pretty sight."

"Maybe he deserved it," Jack snapped.

"Hey, whose camp are you in?"

"Just forget it."

"Sure thing. Boss."

"Why are you here, anyway?"

"You had a phone call. I thought I should let you know right away. Sorry if I interrupted."

"You didn't interrupt anything," Jack lied. He wasn't about to include Ed in his personal business.

Jack returned to his dark office, not bothering to turn on the lights when he entered. He dropped into the chair and glanced at the luminous dial of his watch. Almost midnight. If he was smart, he'd go to bed, but then, he hadn't been very smart tonight. He'd be lucky if Teri ever spoke to him again. His actions hadn't exactly demonstrated professional conduct.

After a few minutes, he rose and crossed the room to retrieve the blueprints from the top of a filing cabinet. Returning to his desk, he clicked on the desk lamp and spread the drawings before him. The more he tried to focus, the more blurry the lines became. He rubbed his eyes in a vain attempt to clear his vision.

Restless, he went to the window. In the winter sky, bright stars were shining. Palm fronds lurched in the steady winds. The temperature had dropped, but Jack thought the heated pool looked inviting in the moonlight. Maybe doing laps would get his mind off of Teri and this mystery.

Chapter Seven

The next morning, Teri sat on the edge of her bed, unable to get Jack out of her thoughts. A date? With Jack? What was she thinking?

Her adrenaline had pumped into overtime when he'd announced his plan. And she'd plunged into the idea without thinking first. It wasn't until Ed broke in on their search and she hurried home that she realized just what she'd committed to.

She groaned out loud. A date with a man whose sultry eyes made her toes curl. The more she spent time with Jack, the more her emotions betrayed her. She'd lose her calm, cool composure and suddenly her heart would race and her palms would grow moist. Boy, was she in serious trouble.

Straightening, she smoothed her navy and white suit. She nodded at herself in the full-length mirror hooked to the closet door. Right now her responsibilities beckoned. Good hard work would sober her thoughts. To prove her point, she ran the comb through thick waves until her scalp hurt, then she hurried off to the hotel.

After a brief meeting with her staff, Teri settled into her comfortable desk chair to sift through paperwork. She hadn't gotten too involved when the intercom buzzed.

"Teri Price."

"Hi, stranger. This is Lisa from Human Resources returning your call."

Teri gripped the handset, a smile playing over her lips. "Thanks for getting back to me. Did you learn anything about the contractor or the abandoned wing?"

"Not much, I'm afraid. The last manager didn't keep very good files so I couldn't find any documentation here. You'll have to check on your end. And there's no record of who issued the request to remodel the wing. But what's really odd is that there are some papers missing."

Alarm shot through Teri. "Papers?"

"History of work done at West Wind. We've gotten most of the paper history of the properties owned by Hotels, Inc. on the computer. Since West Wind was built in the early part of the nineteen hundreds, it's understandable that records might be lost. You might want to check a storage room or someplace where the previous owners kept old documents," Lisa paused for a moment, her voice muffled, then returned to the conversation. "I have in front of me notations made by the entry clerk regarding remodeling a few years back, listing the dates and pertinent information."

Teri scrambled to find a pen and blank piece of stationary. "Anything current?"

She heard the rustle of papers over the line before Lisa spoke. "No. Some type of upgrading work is done every year, although major remodeling jobs occur every five years or so, depending on the property."

"What about the Jacaranda wing?"

"That's the weird thing. It's not mentioned as a current job or even a future project."

Teri's mind worked furiously to come up with answers, but there were none. If Lisa didn't have a written job order, odds were there wasn't one. Unless someone took it. But why?

Lisa spoke again, her voice lowered. "Oh, and some friendly words of advice."

Warning churned in Teri's stomach. "Go ahead."

Mr. Kramer got wind of my search. He wanted specifics, but I played dumb."

"Lisa, please don't get in trouble because of me."

"Don't worry, he's out of town for a few days, so I'm in the clear. Besides, I'm intrigued now. I've always loved a good mystery."

Lisa promised to fax Teri the information she did have. Still, the questions loomed. Why would someone want a history of West Wind? And what about the remodeling? She didn't have much information, but at least it was a start.

By six o'clock that evening she was far from ready for the date. Jack strode into her office wearing a tuxedo and looking incredibly dashing. His sun-bleached hair looked almost white against the black suit, his tanned face more handsome than ever. The smile on his lips when he entered the room died as he looked her over.

"You're still in work clothes."

"I know," she said, rushing around her desk to retrieve the dress, protected in a garment bag hanging behind the door. "Sorry. I can change in a minute."

He pulled back a snowy white cuff and glanced at his gold watch. "Sorry, no time. We're supposed to be at my parents by seven. They've invited a few people over for drinks before the ball. As it is, we'll just make it on time."

She stared at him, aghast. "I can't go like this!"

He took the vinyl bag and draped it over his arm. "You can change there," he said, grabbing her arm and leading her to his truck.

Jack remained quiet as he drove, moving through beach traffic as they crossed the palm-lined causeway. The day had warmed as Florida weather often does in the winter. Teri rolled down the window, breathing in the salty air, hoping to calm her nerves.

Once on the mainland, they drove several miles through a busy commercial area before reaching an affluent neighborhood. Stately houses decorated with tropical plants and symmetrically shaped hedges adorned a quiet side street. The damp scent of freshly mowed grass tickled her nostrils as the rhythmic hissing of sprinkler systems soothed her nerves after a long day of commotion.

Minutes later, the truck passed through a decorative front gate. She glanced at Jack.

A sprawling house loomed before her. A grand doorway with etched-glass panels graced the entrance, dim windows flanked either side. Palm trees and thick green plants decorated the grounds.

"Nice place," she commented in a quiet voice.

"Yeah."

"Your folks live here?"

"Yeah."

Oh boy.

Jack parked alongside several BMWs and a Mercedes. Teri sighed. This was going to be a long night.

Jack led her to the front door, where he stopped to ring the bell.

"Don't you just walk into your own house?"

"It's my parent's house. I don't live here."

She opened her mouth to ask what difference that made, when the door swung open and an older version of Jack stood at the threshold.

"Hello, Dad."

"Jack." He turned to Teri, his brow raised with surprise. "Your mother was under the impression you'd be here alone."

Shaking his father's hand, Jack introduced Teri. "We've been spending a lot of time together lately, and I thought she'd enjoy the ball. She's a history buff."

Teri stepped up to the door. "Pleased to met you, Mr. Bishop."

"Please, call me Roy." He eyed the garment bag she

held, then motioned them inside. "Why don't you go out back and meet the rest of the family."

They walked through the elegantly appointed living room that led to a huge screened-in patio. An in-ground pool glistened, the center point of the patio. Candles set in floating lilies skimmed over the water. Pungent citronella torches burned in discrete locations, casting wavering shadows in the corners of the porch. Several people stood by the calm, clear pool, holding drinks and making conversation. Teri caught the scent of gardenia mingled with the aroma of Jack's spicy cologne and grew light–headed.

"Jack, over here," waved an older woman wearing a jade gown dripping in sequins. Teri clutched the garment bag containing her simple chiffon dress.

"Mom," Jack whispered out of the corner of his mouth before taking Teri's hand and walking over.

His mother's brow furrowed when she finally glimpsed Teri. "Who have we here?" she asked, giving Teri the once over.

"My date for the ball tonight," he said as he leaned over to peck his mother's cheek. "I'd like you to meet Teri Price."

Undercurrents pricked at her and intensified when Jack slipped his arm around her waist. With great reluctance, she slipped into "date" mode.

Soon his two brothers with wife and fiancée joined the group, all dressed in formal dress clothes, openly curious about Teri. That left one gorgeous blond woman standing at the pool's edge, twisting a drink in her hand, a scowl wrinkling her very made-up brow.

"My dear," Mary Bishop laid her hand on Teri's arm. "I'm afraid your attire will never do. This is a formal affair."

"Teri worked late, Mother. If you don't mind she'll change here."

"Oh, of course," Mary grudgingly agreed. "Please, make yourself at home."

Teri tried to move away, but Jack tugged her to him. She glanced up a him and saw desperation in his eyes. He was clearly up to something.

Mary spoke to her son. "Jack, dear, you remember Tina Hayes? She couldn't wait to see you again."

The warning signals struck again when Jack's hand clenched her shoulder. It didn't take much to put two and two together and realize that Jack's mother had invited this woman to be his date. No wonder Mary was surprised to meet her.

The blond woman sashayed up to Jack, practically purring in his ear. She wore a silver gown that looked like it had been made especially for her. "It's been a while, Jack. You still look wonderful."

Jack pulled Teri closer to his side. He squeezed so hard the air rushed out of her. She pinched his hand, hoping he'd release her. He only hugged her tighter.

"You look . . . better than in high school."

Tina pouted at his awkward compliment. "Still not a man of many words, I see."

"That's right." He gazed down at Teri, a grimace on his face. "Do you want a drink?"

"Please," she muttered. Once he released her she

moved away from the crowd to the far side of the pool, taking a deep calming breath.

Jack appeared at her side, extending a glass of sparkling water toward her. She accepted it, careful to sip the cold, crisp beverage slowly, while questions brewed in her mind.

"So," she asked. "What's with the old girlfriend?"

Jack eyebrow arched. "Old girlfriend?"

"Tina is one, isn't she?"

Jack had the grace to look embarrassed. "Yeah."

"You knew she'd be here, didn't you?"

"I had my suspicions."

"That explains all the attention you're lavishing on me." She paused, hating the catch in her voice. "You ambushed me, Jack. Why didn't you warn me?"

"Because it doesn't matter. You're my date."

She didn't know what to say. His attention didn't stray to Tina like most guys' would. He kept his gaze on her alone. In an odd way, it made her feel special.

Jack took a swig of his drink. He stared at the pool, the candle flames reflected in his eyes. After a moment, he looked at her. "You're right. I should have told you. I guess I wanted to get the point across to my mother that she shouldn't play matchmaker."

Not much of an apology, she thought. But it was probably the best she'd get.

"So, are you my date?"

She remained mute, letting him sweat a little as he waited for her answer. It was the least he deserved.

"Please," he insisted. "Let the old girlfriend know I'm off limits." Teri didn't appreciate being a buffer,

but like it or not, she was here. Might as well have
fun in the process. Besides, she'd never been the other
woman before. This night just might turn out to be a
major source of entertainment.

She narrowed her eyes and pursed her lips, trying
to act stern when she really planned on milking the
situation.

"Sure, I'll help you. But by the time I'm finished,
you'll think twice about asking me for another favor."

Chapter Eight

Teri excused herself and hurried to the bathroom. Although she looked much the way she did twelve hours earlier, dressed for work, inspiration now made her bold. She released her hair from the binding clip, bent over and ran her fingers through the mass, then threw her head back. Now she looked windblown instead of corporate.

Next, she pulled a make-up kit from her purse. She darkened the eyeliner and mascara, highlighted her cheekbones and applied fresh lipstick. She smiled at her handy work. Now she looked dramatic—a match for any old girlfriend.

She tossed her weapons back into the purse. Now, the moment of truth. She zipped open the bag, expecting to see the blue chiffon dress she'd picked out at the hotel boutique. Instead, she pulled out a black, beaded minidress. Her mouth fell open. What happened to her dress?

Tom. It had to be Tom. He'd come into the boutique when she was deciding on a dress and cast his vote for the beaded number. Said Jack would like the minidress better. Apparently her assistant had taken it upon himself to switch bags.

She searched the bag, but the only other items inside were a pair of silk hose and matching strappy sandals.

There was even a jewelers box containing diamond earrings and a pendant. Goodness, she was supposed to *wear* this ensemble?

Her heart beat in panic. Either this was a mix-up, or Tom set out to sabotage her night. Someone, somewhere, must be wearing her dress tonight. Holding the dress up in the light, Teri laughed. This was not her.

But she could picture Jack picking it out . . . maybe Tom wasn't in on this little switch alone.

After changing out of her suit, Teri gently took hold of the dress and lowered it over her head. The material shimmied down her body. She glanced at her image, again stunned. The dress fit snugly. The cap sleeves glittered in the bathroom light.

Taking a deep breath, she carefully placed on the jewelry. The diamond pendant glittered against her skin. If she played her cards right, Jack's thoughts wouldn't wander far from her tonight. Especially to the old girlfriend in the silver dress.

She packed up her work clothes, fluffed her hair once more, and headed back to the group. Once she spotted Jack, she headed right for him, intending to break up his little tête-à-tête with Tina. She slipped her hand through his arm. "I'm back, darling. Catching up on old times?"

Jack stiffened at her touch, but when he looked at her, his eyes grew wide with surprise. She smiled and tilted her head, awaiting his answer.

His voice cracked. "There's not much to catch up on."

Tina pouted. "Don't be silly, Jack. Remember the prom?"

Teri thought Jack was too busy inspecting the 'new her' from head to toe to remember anything. She liked his dazed expression.

Tina prodded on. She tugged at Jack's sleeve. "Jack, did you hear me?"

"It was a long time ago."

Jack removed Teri's hand from his arm and wrapped her snugly against him. "You look unbelievable," he breathed in her ear.

"Guess black's really your favorite color?"

"Sure beats matron blue."

"Was this your idea or Tom's?"

"Both. Hope you don't mind. I know what these people expect." His gaze lingered over her again. "Looks better on you than I thought."

Mary Bishop joined them, her gaze lighting on Jack's arm draped over her shoulders. Teri nestled into Jack's embrace, catching the scent of cologne that lingered on his shirt.

"So, you two met at the hotel?" Mary asked.

"Yes," they answered in unison. Teri looked up at

his face, almost giggling at the devilish twinkle in Jack's eyes.

Mary doggedly continued. "Jack hasn't mentioned you to us."

Jack stared into Teri's eyes. "Some things are better left unsaid."

It's an act, Teri reminded herself. *Don't let his smooth words push you off guard.*

Much as her mind drilled the reality in her, her heart still beat uncontrollably. She almost wished circumstances could be different, that they could have a real relationship. But she couldn't forget their goal, the mystery back at West Wind.

"What is your position at the hotel?" Mary asked, interrupting her thoughts.

Teri answered politely, hoping to ease the tension.

After a few more minutes of questions, Jack excused them and carried their drinks to a secluded corner of the patio, only to stare at her.

"What?"

"Where's the real Teri Price? I know I drove over with her, but she's missing and a gorgeous woman in a fancy dress has taken her place."

"You really like it?"

His smile faded. "You really don't realize how great you look, do you?"

Words escaped her. She'd been a little unsure when she slipped on this dress, but suddenly tonight felt like prom night, full of magical wonder and excitement. And she intended to enjoy the entire ball, because she'd never attended her own high school dance.

"Your family seems nice," she commented.

"Yeah."

"Lovely house."

"Yeah."

"We're down to mono-syllables again?"

Jack glanced at her, his eyebrow raised. "I'm doing that?"

Teri chuckled. "Yeah."

"Okay, I get the point. I'm just awestruck over you."

"Don't go overboard, Jack. You act as though I was some dowdy old thing before tonight."

He rubbed his forehead, then reclined back into the wrought iron chair, his legs stretched out and crossed at the ankles. "Sorry. I didn't mean that. You just caught me off guard." Staring over the group of laughing family members, his eyes narrowed. "I hope you don't mind their meddling."

"It's no big deal. All the better families hire me for cocktail conversation."

He smiled, reluctantly at first, then with real humor. She was beginning to read the subtle changes that were Jack. "Thanks for helping me out tonight. You know, for one uptight manager, you sure know how to make me laugh."

"It's all those psychology courses I took in college. They help me with my people-handling skills."

He grinned and his eyes flashed. "Do I need to be handled?"

She laughed, enjoying the banter. "Most definitely."

Jack unfolded his fist and clasped her hand in his.

The night sounds dimmed and the wavering candle light cast romantic shadows around them. Conversation dwindled to murmurs, but her heart pounded loudly in her ears.

Once again she found herself lost in the nearness of Jack. He was a problem she knew she'd have to straighten out soon—they had a job in common, and she couldn't let their work relationship suffer from this pleasurable interlude.

"So, Miss Price, you think you can handle me? Or should I say *us*?" The husky timbre sent another surge of warning through her.

She exhaled a shaky breath. She was getting in too deep. Much as she wanted to say yes, that they were starting something special, she knew she had to stay strong. For her job. For the good of the hotel. "I don't think this is a good idea."

An understatement if there ever was one. With all the craziness at the hotel, she needed him as an ally and nothing more.

She extracted her hand from Jack's grasp and stood. Mumbling "excuse me," she dashed into the house. Once inside the brightly lit kitchen, she sought to regain her sanity. What was she thinking? Jack serious about her? No, it had to be the romantic ambiance and her active imagination.

Taking an empty glass from the counter, she filled it with cold tap water and took a long drink.

"Enjoying yourself?" asked a rigid female voice behind her.

Teri swung around to face Jack's mother. "Yes, thank you. I can't wait for the ball."

Mary nodded. "You and Jack seem to be close."

Right to the point, Teri thought.

"I must admit," Mary continued, "when we were first introduced, I had my doubts. Jack always was fickle when it came to girlfriends. I can't recall the last time he brought a woman friend home."

Teri could understand why.

"Anyway, after watching you two alone, I can see the sparks between you."

"Sparks?" Teri croaked.

"Oh yes, it's quite obvious."

The older woman had opened the freezer, dropping ice cubes into a silver ice bucket. "He must have changed significantly over the past few years. We don't see him often."

Teri thought she detected regret in Mary's voice. It wasn't her place to interfere; she barely knew Jack as it was.

"He really does a good job, then?" his mother asked.

"I'm pleased with his performance."

"That's good to hear. After the fiasco with the agency, I wouldn't want you to depend on him too much."

"What fiasco?"

Mary's eyebrow rose. "He hasn't told you?"

"No. I'm only aware of his reputation with Hotels, Inc."

"Then you'll have to ask him."

Teri remember Jack's remark about his family's opinion of him. "I'm sure I will."

Jack grew concerned when Teri didn't return.

You scared her off, Bishop.

He stared into the crystal water of the pool, wishing he could conjure up images of the future. Wondering what place he held in Teri's life. Wondering if she was, at this moment, inside calling a taxi.

The thing he feared most had come to pass: he'd grown wildly attracted to Teri, and now she returned the sentiment. He knew it when he touched her, and tonight they'd almost admitted it with words. It wasn't a game, and it wasn't one-sided. They were on the same wavelength. If he'd learned anything tonight, he knew they were headed for disaster if they gave in to a personal relationship. He had a job to do here, to make his reports, and it didn't include a romantic entanglement with the source of his current assignment. And if she found out, she'd never forgive him.

He was as certain of that as he was that something odd was going on at West Wind.

He glanced at the house just as his mother stepped from the kitchen. Teri moved into view at the pass-through window. With her hair down and her face brightened with make-up, she didn't resemble the workaholic woman he worked with. He doubted she was even aware of her allure. But he was.

He headed into the house and found her in the kitchen.

"Hey, you all right? I got worried when you didn't come back. Besides, you left me alone with Tina."

"Scary thought," she replied with a false shiver.

"Hey, there's been some weird things going on lately. Nothing would surprise me."

"I must be slacking on the job."

"Not yet. So, are you okay?"

"Yes. I was having an interesting conversation with your mother."

"That couldn't have been good."

"Actually, it was quite enlightening."

"Okay, spill. What'd she say?"

"She mentioned something about your job at the agency."

Jack froze. "She didn't give you details?"

"No, she said to ask you."

Great. Now he had to decide. If Teri wanted the information, she could find out. Perhaps it was best for him to fill her in. "I worked for a large PI firm in Tampa. About two years into the job I headed sur veillance on a case involving a client who thought his wife was having an affair."

Teri placed her glass on the counter. "Was she?"

Jack rubbed the back of his neck. "Yeah. I filed my report and thought the job was finished. A week later the guy murdered his wife."

"How awful."

"The guy was a big-time lawyer, so the local news stories were endless. I didn't handle the press well, which ticked off my boss. He put the blame on my shoulders, and since I figured he was right, I quit."

Jack grew uncomfortable under Teri's scrutiny. Just like he felt those years ago when the press hounded him. "Jack, it wasn't your fault. How could you know what that man would do?"

"I've always thought I could have done more. Checked the guy's profile better, maybe watch them after the case closed."

"You did your job. Second guessing won't change the events, or your part in it. Forgive yourself and move on."

"Just like you have about the Daytona problem?"

Teri's eyes flashed. "Then I guess we both have to work on forgiving ourselves for the past."

A few moments of quiet passed between them until Teri spoke again. "How did corporate come to hire you?"

"You know Marcus King, CEO of Hotels, Inc.?"

"Not personally."

"He's a family friend. I played football with his son in high school, then in college. We always got along well, and when Marcus heard about my mess, he called to check up on me. Once I felt like I could handle another job, Marcus hired me. Not long after that he offered me the head of security position. I jumped at the opportunity. The job required travel, and eventually I got tired of the constant running to one place or another and decided I wanted to settle down." Jack smiled at the memory. "Marcus tried to talk me out of my decision, but when he realized how serious I was, he turned around and helped me get my firm started. That's how I got the West Wind job."

"We certainly need you."

"Thanks for the vote of confidence."

"I wouldn't tell you this if it weren't true. You're good at your job."

"So are you."

Teri grinned. "Hmm . . . looks like we have a mutual admiration society going on here."

"Remember that when we get to the ball tonight. We're there to work the room."

"Jack, that doesn't sound like much fun."

"Tonight's not about fun."

Her eyebrow rose. "Really? Because I recall you telling me to lighten up. And since we're all dressed up with somewhere to go, I figured this was as good a time as any to relax."

He chuckled. "You set me up for that one."

"Yes, I did. Now you know what your relentless badgering sounds like."

"Hey, I don't badger. I make observations."

"Well, my observations tell me that you're the one who needs to relax."

Jack ran his hand over his face. "I wish it was so simple. I just keep getting these—I guess, hunches, for lack of a better word. Tonight we'll be with people who really know the history of this area, so we've got to pay attention."

Teri thought about her phone call with Lisa. She'd been concerned about the missing records. Now was their chance to fill in the blanks.

"You're right. We are working. But promise me one thing."

"Name it."

"At least let me have one dance tonight. For fun."

Jack leaned back, hitting the counter with his hip. How could he resist when she asked him so sweetly?

"One for fun."

Teri's face lit up with pure delight. They stared at each other for long static minutes. Teri's hold over him seemed to be working overtime.

"Come along, you two," Mary called, her tone brisk as she entered the kitchen. "You can ogle each other at the ball."

Jack shot his mother a look, then turned his attention to Teri. She was blushing and she looked ready to run.

The guests filed from the patio and headed trough the living room before breaking off to separate vehicles. Jack heard his brother's laughter.

"Yeah, buddy. Save all that serious stuff for later."

Jack nearly groaned out loud and stepped into the hallway. "Thanks for the advice."

"Any time." More laughter followed.

"C'mon, Teri, let's—Teri?"

His eyes searched the kitchen.

Teri was gone.

Chapter Nine

Jack found her by the truck. She was leaning against the tailgate, staring into the night. Worried by her abrupt departure, he grasped her shoulders and turned her to face him. "Hey, what's up?"

She grabbed his lapels and buried her face inside his jacket. Her muffled voice sent vibrations against his jacket. "Just embarrassed. Nothing a bottle of strychnine won't cure."

"Teri, this isn't a big deal. It's not like they've never seen me talking to a woman before. Hey, at least I wasn't kissing you."

Her head popped up, hitting his chin. As his head jerked back, he bit his tongue.

"You make a habit of kissing women in front of your parents?"

He dabbed at his tongue, relieved there was no

blood. "Of course I don't make a *habit* of it. I just meant that you shouldn't be embarrassed."

His family chose that moment to leave the house for the ball. Mary carried out Teri's garment bag, and handed it to Jack. He ushered Teri into the cab of the truck, then jogged around to the driver's side. "Let's just forget anything happened and remember our job tonight."

"How much farther?" she asked ten minutes later.

"We're not too far. The society reserved the grand ballroom at the Belleview Biltmore Hotel."

Teri shook her head. "Talk about history. Those two hotels alone have more history than we can imagine."

"Yeah. And these folks love to spout off all the history they know. We should learn something helpful tonight."

Jack pulled up before the grand entrance, surrendering his keys to the valet. He hooked Teri's arm through his as they entered the Victorian hotel. He walked slowly so that she could take in all the beautiful antique furniture and potted plants before entering the ballroom. At the door, he produced his invitation and they passed through the threshold, into a fantasy world of twinkling lights and shimmering gold.

Teri gasped in audible delight. Jack smiled, enjoying her reaction. Her hand flew to her neck and she twisted the pendant between her fingers.

Before long new introductions were made. He was proud of Teri, as she gracefully pried more details out of unsuspecting men that he would have guessed. With the way she was going, he wouldn't leave her alone for fear that some single guy would monopolize her time.

"Jack, how good of you to come." The president of the society, Milton Newborn, and his wife approached him.

Jack smiled, shaking the older man's hand and nodding to his wife. "As if my mother would have let me stay home."

Milton chuckled. "Mary does have a way of twisting one's arm."

Small talk continued for a few moments before Teri started to ask questions. "This is a lovely hotel, but we're rather partial to West Wind. Has the society thought about using our hotel for a future function?"

A shadow passed over Mrs. Newborn's eyes and her husband looked uncomfortable. Jack glanced at Teri as she looked up at him. He recognized the question in her eyes and answered with the barest shrug of his shoulders.

"Did I say something wrong?" she asked.

"No, my dear," Milton assured her. "Mrs. Newborn's family had some bitter history with West Wind. An old family misfortune they wish to forget."

The Newborns excused themselves and moved on. "I hope I didn't put my foot in too far," Teri said, watching the stately couple move on.

"I wouldn't worry about it. You asked a perfectly innocent question."

Worry marred her forehead. "I hope so."

"Jack, I see you spoke with Milton." His mother glided up in a cloud of perfume. Jack stifled a cough.

"Yes, we spoke. By the way, what kind of old family history would get Mrs. Newborn bent out of shape when we mentioned West Wind?"

Mary put her hands over her mouth for a moment. "Did she mention it?"

"No, Teri did. They took off after that."

"It's not a big deal really, but they like to pretend it was a family scandal. Way back in the 1920's someone robbed the family jewelry store. It was rumored to be Al Capone."

Jack couldn't believe his ears. "You're kidding?"

"You know I don't kid, Jack. It's the truth. Apparently the family went to the hotel to try to retrieve the jewelry, but the owners turned them away. They've been bitter ever since."

Roy appeared at that moment to ask his wife for a dance, and Mary swept onto the floor like a debutante.

Jack took Teri's hand. "Shall we?"

Her eyes glittered like gems. "I thought you'd never ask."

As the band set a moderate tempo Jack wished they'd play a slow, jazzy tune. But he couldn't complain. He held Teri in his arms, and hoped she'd stay there all night.

An appealing blush swept over Teri's cheeks. "I think we hit pay dirt with the Newborns."

"Is work all you think about?"

"Hey, you told to me to concentrate on getting information, so I am. Besides, you have to admit, the coincidence is too much. Jack, this is exciting. We now have another story corroborating Martin's. We're on the right track, I can feel it."

"Let's say we change the conversation."

"To what?"

"You. Me. The future."

Her mouth formed an O.

"What, no comment?"

"Sorry. I've gotten so caught up in the sleuthing, you took me by surprise."

Jack twirled her around. Teri's dress sparkled in the dim lighting, but nothing compared to her bright eyes and flushed cheeks. He'd never held a more vibrant woman in his arms.

"Maybe that's our problem. We're so busy finding answers that we haven't spent time learning about each other."

Teri's smile was dazzling. "So, let me get this straight. We've got our info, so now we focus on each other?"

"Sounds like a plan."

"Okay. We'll start simple. Let's see . . . I have a killer review next week, there are strange noises in the hotel, and I have a goal to get to Paris. Plus, one bothersome security guy keeps butting into my job. Does that cover everything?"

"No. Something is missing."

"Missing?"

"How do you feel right this moment?"

"Wonderful. Glorious. Like I'm dancing in a glittering fairyland with my Prince Charming."

Did she even realize what she'd just said? Prince Charming? A figure of speech, he rationalized. Nothing to do with reality.

As they whirled to the music, Jack's heart began to beat a little harder. From the exertion or the woman? He didn't want to examine it too closely, only knew he didn't want this dance to end any time soon.

"How about you? How do you feel?" Teri asked.

"About the same. Except I put holding a beautiful woman in my arms number one on my list."

"Now you make me sound shallow, thinking only about myself."

"I didn't mean to. I've decided I want your focus on me, not your job. And when I want something, I can be pretty single-minded."

She grinned. "That doesn't sound good for me."

He returned a wolfish grin of his own. "Just wait before you decide. Tonight could be the best night of your life."

Her eyes turned dreamy. "I think you might be right."

Teri rested her head on his shoulder and Jack tucked her tightly into his embrace. Other dancers swirled around them to the stirring music. A romantic cocoon wrapped around them, and together their hearts beat as one.

But what would happen after tonight? Jack wondered. What kind of future could they have together? They both seemed to want different things.

That is, until they fell into each other's arms. Then

Jack sensed they were of one mind and heart. Would it last? Could they make it work?

The music flowed from one languid song to another. Jack led her around the room with practiced ease. Teri held on as if he were her life preserver, anchoring her in an ocean of doubt. But could he keep her safe emotionally? Even he couldn't answer that.

"I need something to drink," he muttered, angry at the direction of his thoughts.

When they reached the refreshment table, Jack pushed a cup of cool punch into Teri's hand.

"So," she asked, "what happens next?"

Jack took another drink.

"More research?"

"Guess that leaves out discussing the future."

"I think we should leave that for another time."

She reached out to place her hand on his arm as Martin approached to ask for a dance.

"You mind?" Teri asked Jack, her voice unsure.

He nodded to the floor. "Go ahead. I'll wait here."

Teri made small talk with Martin, but most of the glimmer of the night had faded. Why had Jack acted so interested in them as a couple, then seemed to shy away from the idea? If she wasn't already confused by Jack's attitude and the events at the hotel, she might be ready to pretend none of this had happened.

The remainder of the night flew by. By midnight Teri was exhausted and wanted to go home and bury herself under the covers of her cozy bed.

Jack's eyes narrowed when she returned to his side after a final turn around the floor with his father.

"What do you say I take you home?"

She nodded with relief.

As the valet retrieved Jack's truck, she shivered in the starless night. The wind had picked up as the temperature dropped, dragging a chill off the Gulf.

Jack slipped off his jacket and draped it over her shoulders. She snuggled into the warmth, drawing the lapel over her nose to inhale his cologne.

Both were silent on the drive back to the hotel. Teri stared out the window as shapeless shadows rushed by. Her life had been so predictable, so . . . boring until she met Jack. He turned her carefully–planned life upside down and inside out.

Before tonight, her review was the only obstacle in her plans for the future. She was so close to her goal of getting to Paris. Why did she have to meet Jack now?

Then again, maybe Paris was a pipe dream. Maybe she was supposed to be here. At West Wind. In Jack's life.

A cloud passed, revealing the moon in an otherwise dark night. She sunk deeper into the jacket, closer to the warmth that had come from Jack's body.

They reached the hotel minutes later. Jack helped her out of the truck, handing her the garment bag.

Teri shrugged off his jacket and handed it to him. "Thanks."

He took it, his hand brushing hers. They stood in awkward silence.

Flinging the jacket over his shoulder, Jack said, "About tonight—"

"I think it would be best if we concentrate on the hotel right now. Once we get answers, then we can focus on us. If there is an us."

Teri watched as a flash of emotion passed over Jack's face. He spoke quietly. "I agree. For now."

She almost laughed. He appeared as confused as she felt.

She wanted more of a commitment from Jack, but it was too soon for anything more. She wondered what path the journey would lead them down.

She didn't want to give her heart to him and find out later that he wasn't serious about her. She couldn't bear that. She'd be better off in Paris. Alone.

"I'll see you tomorrow."

He pushed his free hand into his pants pocket. "Tomorrow."

Teri sat in her car long after Jack went into the hotel. Finally she turned the key. As she put the car in reverse, she thought she glimpsed a faint light in her rear view mirror, coming from a room on the first floor of the Jacaranda wing. She pressed the brake pedal and waited.

Nothing. No light. Only darkness.

Focusing on her driving, Teri steered her car out of the parking lot. If she'd looked back in her mirror one more time, she'd have seen the beam of light again.

Chapter Ten

In just the space of a day the temperature had turned cooler as clouds gathered in the sky. A group of determined vacationers from the north braved the chilly waters of the pool. The waves hit the beach harder than usual, creating a frothy shoreline, but a couple of children scoured the sand for seashells and lost trinkets.

Teri kept to herself most of the day, not ready to face Jack after declaring that the mystery of the hotel took precedence over any type of personal relationship between them. By the time she gathered her belongings to head home, the night had long settled its dark blanket over the hotel. After a knock on her door, Tom poked his head into her office.

"Mr. Bishop called a few minutes ago. He had some pressing business to take care of, so he won't be back tonight."

"Did he ask to speak to me?"

"No, he only wanted me to relay the message."

Unreasonably hurt that he hadn't spoken to her directly, Teri tamped down the heavy-hearted ache. "Thanks." Then, as Tom stepped back, she said, "By the way, Tom, great job on handling the front desk. I've been busy and your help has been invaluable."

With stunned confusion written on his face, Tom scratched his tousled brown hair. "Thanks, Miss Price."

"Call me Teri."

Surprise crossed his face and he nodded uncertainly.

As soon as Tom left, her thoughts returned to Jack. She had no idea where to get in touch with him. Was he embarrassed to see her after their heart-to-heart last night? The only way she'd know for sure was to talk to him, but he'd made himself scarce. She sighed. There was always tomorrow.

For the first time in a long time, Teri actually looked forward to going home. She'd put on a pair of comfortable pajamas and fuzzy slippers, then settle in front of the television, relaxing in her cozy armchair with a handmade afghan wrapped around her. Or maybe she'd turn on the stereo and get immersed in a good book. The options were endless, even if they didn't include Jack.

On impulse, she picked up a novel in the hotel gift shop. A romance novel of all things! Jack would be pleased with her romantic change of heart.

Juggling her briefcase, purse, and a take-out dinner, she went out to her car. Tonight the chef had prepared her all-time favorite, shrimp scampi, and sent her a plate. Her mouth watered as the buttery aroma teased her nose.

After unlocking her small sedan, she tossed in her belongings and gingerly laid her dinner on the passenger seat. A strong wind blew overhead. The air had steadily cooled all afternoon, and the damp Florida night cut to the bone. Shivering, she buttoned her jacket before stepping into the car. As she did, a dark shadow passed her peripheral vision.

She straightened quickly, in time to see someone disappear around the corner of the main building, heading in the direction of the Jacaranda wing.

Adrenaline pumped through her veins and her heart beat madly. Surely she hadn't imagined this. She scanned the employee parking lot, only to find it deserted. The waves crashing against the beach were the only sounds she heard. Palm trees swayed as the wind picked up, the fronds like spindly fingers in the shadows. Above, stars were obscured by swiftly gathering clouds in the winter sky. She was alone with the dark silhouette.

It could be a guest, she reasoned, *but why would anyone slink by, as if they were afraid to be seen?*

Chills ran down her spine. She thought about the strange noises they'd been investigating. A coincidence? Crossing her arms to ward off the eerie feeling that came over her, Teri's heart screamed not to follow the ghostly shape, but her mind countered otherwise. Did she have time to get help? To call the police?

They would arrive with lights flashing, and upset the guests. Could she risk the publicity?

Her instincts were right. This was her chance to find out who haunted the empty wing, even to solve the mystery. What a score for her job review.

She quietly closed and locked the car door, then pocketed the keys. If the temperature hadn't fallen so low tonight, she would've been tempted to remove her shoes.

Trying to appear as unobtrusive as possible, Teri hurried to the side of the building. She eased down along the long wall of the building to cautiously peek around the corner.

No one.

Turning to get a glimpse of the empty parking lot one last time, she took a deep breath and stepped around the corner. Darkness enveloped her as the street lights disappeared on this side of the hotel. The bright lights from the parking area that had illuminated her path only seconds ago were now effectively snuffed out as the structure loomed over her. She tugged her jacket closer in an attempt to keep the chilly draft at bay. Her legs shook, but she wasn't sure if it came from the nipping wind or her fear. She knew one thing for sure, though: Jack would skin her alive if he knew what she was up to.

When she reached the far end and rounded the corner, she hesitated for a moment, aware that she saw no movement since starting this hunt. Her gut instinct spurred her on. She peered around the corner. Nothing. Street lights once again flashed dimly as the trees moved in the breeze, but no other moving shadows. Puzzled, she leaned back against the wall. She *knew* she'd witnessed someone lurking about. Had she lost her prey so easily?

Her heart's pounding diminished marginally. She strained her eyes to see anything unusual in the darkness. The night once again concealed any clues that would be obvious in the light of day. Disappointment shot through her.

After waiting for what seemed like hours and detecting no further movement, Teri decided she must be mistaken. There was no prowler. Her eyes were playing tricks on her already kindled imagination. She wanted to find a culprit of some sort, needed to if she were to prove that she could handle this hotel, or another more prestigious location. She dropped her head back against the cold wall to stare into the murky sky. So much for her great powers of deduction.

The unusually cold air seeped into her clothes. She rubbed her shaking hands together before pushing away from the building. As she retraced the path back to her car, a sudden gust of wind sucked a section of curtain through a partially–open sliding glass door—a door to a hotel room that should have been locked up tight.

Teri froze. So she *had* seen something suspicious. All the doors on the unused floor were kept locked, especially since they expected a contractor to turn this area into a construction zone.

Tiptoeing toward the door, she timidly pushed the handle. Tight at first, the door refused to budge further in the track. She put all her weight behind a final thrust. Gradually, it slid all the way open. The curtain billowed out again as the wind caught the hem, reaching out to her. Teri briefly closed her eyes and took a deep breath. She'd come too far to turn back now.

With a burst of confidence, she slipped through the opening and stepped inside the room. It took long seconds for her eyes to focus in the deep darkness. Sudden silence roared in her ears. A musty smell replaced the clean night air. She tried to make out any familiar object and wished desperately for a flashlight. On second thought, that would only alert the intruder to her presence. She'd rely only on her heightened senses to guide her.

Even with outstretched hands, she bumped into a chair. She ran her fingertips over the wall's rough surface as she stumbled forward. Using careful steps, she reached the door, turned the knob, and quickly slipped into the hallway.

Her sight grew accustomed to the dimness. She could make out shapes, varying shades of black and gray, but shapes nonetheless. Her confidence soared. If she could see just the tiniest bit, then perhaps she'd find the intruder.

She strained to hear any telltale sounds, but only loud silence greeted her. She stayed put, with her palms flat against the wall. Now what?

Cautiously, she proceeded to the next room. Feeling her way to the open door, she peered inside. Empty. She worked her way into the next three rooms with the same results. Nothing.

I must be crazy, she thought, frustrated with her slow progress. *Only a fool would be sneaking around an empty hotel wing late at night, seeking a ghostly prowler.*

She decided to return to the first room and leave the building when she heard the distinctive tapping sound. Her heart jumped and fear overwhelmed her, but she'd come too far to turn back.

She leaned into the wall beside the entrance to another room. Lost in the darkness, she couldn't determine from which direction the noises originated. She waited patiently, and this time was rewarded with the muffled sound of deep male voices. She couldn't decipher the mumbled words, but one fact became crystal clear: two different voices came from the room.

The jeopardy of the situation registered in Teri's brain. She began to sweat. Afraid to make any kind of movement, she stayed still.

Think! Think! she silently yelled to herself. *Now what am I going to do with two people in the room?* Oh God, why hadn't she called the police?

She inhaled a shaky breath and broke out in a cold sweat all over again. Why had she come in here alone?

She stood, sucking in quick gusts of air, and her fear subsided enough for her to think rationally. What would Jack suggest if he were here?

With her muscles taut, Teri couldn't move voluntarily. Her frozen body had taken control of the situation and her mind turned to mush. Where was her infamous control now that she needed it?

When her breathing calmed, Teri concentrated on

the voices, noting the distinct differences now that she inched closer. While the words remained undistinguishable, the volume and tone grew more sharp and high-pitched as they reached the level of a full blown argument.

Focusing on the voices, Teri stepped to the door. She gripped the door frame and peeked into the room. Flashlights moved willy-nilly across the room at odd angles. Once again she could only make out shapes, but these were more human looking than anything she had seen so far.

"Hey," one voice said. "This room is clean. Let's get going."

"Wait," said the other. "We have to be certain."

Teri's skin prickled. She recognized that voice. But from where? Desperate to hear more, she edged closer. Before she had a chance to really see anything, a flash of light moved in her direction.

Raw panic penetrated her body. She ran down the hallway, ducked into a room a few doors down and silently closed the door. In the grip of terror, she fell back, hitting her head hard. She groaned. What next?

Self-preservation inspired her. She beat a path across the room to a set of sliding doors. Teri fumbled with the lock, then pulled and pushed and kicked the metal, but the doors remained firmly shut. She glanced around the room for another escape route.

She wondered if she should break the glass. Of course not. The men would hear the shatter and come running. No, she'd wait here until the coast was clear.

She slid between the dank drapes and the cold glass

door and waited. Fear griped her. Her throat tightened, hot and stinging, but she swallowed hard in an attempt to keep control.

The voices subsided, but she still wasn't sure if it was safe to leave the room. In the silence, she thought about what landed her in this mess in the first place. Sheer ambition. Was it really so important that she put herself in this danger? Was any promotion worth this? What did she have to prove? And to whom?

What would Jack say when she told him what she'd done? If she even got out of here in one piece. She finally had a promising relationship with a man, someone she respected and genuinely liked. Never mind that she was wildly attracted to him. Never mind that he made her heart pound when he came into view. Never mind that she found herself thinking about him at the most inopportune moments.

In truth, she was afraid she'd never see him again because of her rash actions. How she wished he were here right now. To protect her. To hold her. To reassure her.

She silently admitted how important Jack had become in her life, and the fear that gnawed at the pit of her stomach just reminded her that she may never see him again.

She brushed her fears aside and stood. After brief seconds, she eased across the room, opened the door and looked out. Nothing. No flashlights, no voices, no footsteps. To get her bearings, she crept across the hallway. Which room had she initially entered through? Once she located the room, she darted inside, immediately bumping into a rock-solid, breathing body.

Chapter Eleven

She screamed.

He screamed.

They both screamed together.

Teri bolted toward the glass doors, adrenaline fueling her escape. Out of the darkness, someone grabbed her around the waist and knocked the air out of her. She kicked and lashed out at the assailant. His flashlight fell to the floor, flickered, then went out, plunging them into darkness. He cursed, lost his balance, and in doing so loosened his hold on her.

Teri sensed her advantage and flung herself toward the door, only to have her feet tangled in something. She reached out to grab a fistful of the curtain to steady her feet, then lurched outside. Falling heavily into the dirt, she landed with a "humph" which turned into a groan as a sharp-edged pain shot up her right arm and into her shoulder blade.

116

Not waiting for the intruder to catch her again, Teri scrambled to her feet, protecting her injured arm. As she caught her breath, she cast a final glimpse toward the door. All she saw in the moon's light was the shape of her attacker, then she ran as fast as she could to the main lobby of the hotel.

She entered the foyer out of breath, barely able to relay her story. The night clerk called security. Ed Raven arrived in minutes, looking harried. He took one look at the scene and called Jack. Tom brought her a glass of cold water. Exhausted, Teri dropped into one of the plush love seats, cradling her bruised arm, determined to appear cool, calm, and collected.

Teri accepted her staff's help, even though she didn't like to be fussed over. As they stared at her oddly, she realized her hair was a mess and the overcoat Tom gave her hung haphazardly off her left shoulder. Removing it with a grimace, she lowered it to her waist then slumped into the comfortable seat. She closed her eyes and folded her trembling fingers tightly together. She needed to catch her breath, needed time to think. There would be a lot of explaining to do.

Especially to Jack, who now entered the building, looking like one irate security expert. He took one look at her and pointed to her office. She gathered the coat and followed him inside.

"Are you nuts or just suicidal?"

"Neither," Teri fumed. "I'm impulsive."

Jack paced the confines of her office, his heart rate beating off the charts. "This is not what I meant when

I suggested you find a new image. I thought relaxing a little would be reasonable. Maybe finding a safe hobby to fill your spare time. I didn't think you wanted to play PI on your own."

"I told you, I'm fine."

When Jack received the call it woke him out of a sound sleep, and he'd been mildly annoyed. Then he found out Teri was involved and he felt the blood turn cold in his veins. *How could she have been so reckless?* He quickly pulled on jeans and a flannel shirt, then raced to be by her side.

Her pale face spoke volumes and her shaky voice confirmed she'd been upset pretty badly.

"I didn't get hurt," she said defensively, while absently rubbing her shoulder.

Jack knew she was hiding the truth from him. He held his breath and counted to ten before he spoke. "You were incredibly lucky. It was a first-time fluke. Beginner's luck."

She lifted her chin as she always did when challenged. "I know you're annoyed, but I got out safely."

"That's a matter of opinion."

She sniffed at his response. "Do we need to go over this again, or can we call it a night?"

"Please. Indulge me one more time." He crossed his arms over his chest to keep from shaking the story out of her.

Teri leaned forward in her chair, resting her elbows on the desk. Her eyes bore into his. "I left work late, and while I was getting into my car I saw someone running around the building. If I'd gone for help, I never would have caught up with him. I had to move fast."

Jack ran his hand through his hair and clenched his jaw so hard it hurt. "Go on."

She shrugged. "So . . . I followed."

Waiting for a more detailed answer seemed futile. Her stubborn streak returned with a vengeance, her eyes flashed with impatience. But Jack had reached the end of his rope. "That's it? That's all you have to say?"

"For tonight." Teri rose stiffly and walked around her desk, stopping to retrieve her overcoat. "You can interrogate me in the morning, Jack. Right now I want something to eat, and then my bed." She stopped directly before him, fatigue evident on her wan face. "Any objections?"

He heard the catch in her voice and his attitude softened. How could he grill her now when she looked ready to fall over? "I'll drive you home."

"No," she protested. "I'm perfectly capable of driving myself home. It's not far."

Jack decided not to argue. Instead he grabbed her coat and held it out for her. She turned, ready for him to guide her arms through the garment, but cried out when she pulled back her left shoulder.

"What's wrong?"

She rubbed her forearm gently, tears glistening in her eyes. "I landed hard when I fell earlier. I must have twisted the wrong way trying to put my hand through the armhole."

"I knew you were hurt." Jack touched her arm gently, but Teri winced. With a sigh, he draped the coat over her shoulders, then turned her toward the door. "You might think you can handle this, but I know how nerves play games on a person. Especially someone who just went through a traumatic ordeal. I'm driving."

She slumped against the door frame. "Fine. Whatever."

He cupped her elbow gently and steered her through the lobby. Curious eyes followed their exit, but Jack ignored them. His only job tonight was to get Teri home, safe and sound. He'd deal with her crazy stunt tomorrow after they'd both had a good night's sleep.

When they arrived at her apartment, Teri excused herself as soon as they entered the living room. She escaped to what he assumed was her bedroom, slamming the door behind her.

Quietly closing the front door, Jack surveyed his surroundings. He had just stepped into the living room when he heard her whimper. He strode to the closed door. "Hey, you okay in there?"

He heard her mumble before the room grew quiet.

He turned into a small living room decorated in muted shades of rose and blue that led to a kitchenette. A table for two sat against the wall, a vase of fresh carnations a welcoming centerpiece. He wandered around the living area, gazing at watercolor paintings hanging on the wall. The entertainment center held a television and stereo. He knelt on one knee to look through the assortment of CD's. Jazz and R&B. He grinned. For someone so uptight, she sure went for funky music. He picked out an artist he liked and popped it into the player.

Soft saxophone tones floated from the speakers. He stood, looking at the overstuffed flowered sofa and matching easy chair. The soft couch looked inviting, so he sat down to wait for Teri. On a nearby table were some framed photographs. Curious, Jack studied them.

An older man smiled out from one picture. Jack assumed it was her father, since the family resemblance was strong. The next showed three smiling girls wearing matching sorority sweatshirts. They pointed at the photographer.

Jack snatched up the frame for a closer inspection. Pretty and wholesome described the two girls, but Teri glowed with self-assurance and humor. Her cheeks were flushed and the teasing twinkle Jack had come to recognize shone in her eyes. What had happened to make her so different now? He replaced the picture, suddenly feeling awkward and out of place. *I'm as bad as a peeping Tom,* he thought. Jumping up, he stood in the center of the room with hands shoved into his jeans pocket, waiting for her return.

Moments later, she emerged from her bedroom dressed in baggy blue sweats and thick socks. She'd washed off her make-up and pulled her hair into a loose ponytail. Stopping momentarily, she looked at him and blinked, as if surprised to see him.

"I thought you were going home."

"I wanted to make sure you were settled in for the night."

Her face suddenly turned pink and he wondered if she was thinking about the heated words back at her office. "I told you I'm okay. You're worse than a hovering nursemaid." She brushed back a few curling tendrils of hair from her face.

He chuckled. "I've never been accused of being *that* before." He shoved his hands deeper into his pockets. "I guess there's a first time for everything."

She stared at him, a slight grin pulling at her lips. "How about a glass of hot milk?"

He grimaced. "I don't think so. How about something less therapeutic and more tasty."

"Milk is good for you," she scolded.

He followed her into the tiny kitchen. "So I'm told, but that doesn't mean I listen to good advice. I'd rather have coffee."

Her eyebrow raised. "You'll be up all night."

He sighed. Sleep would be impossible now. Visions of Teri in a dark room chasing after prowlers were sure to keep him awake for hours. "I'd still rather have coffee."

She shrugged. "It's your decision."

As she prepared their beverages, Teri remained quiet. Jack couldn't help wondering if the danger of the situation had seeped into her consciousness yet. If she let him, he planned to be there when she crashed.

She handed Jack a mug with the steaming brew and carried her own filled with warm milk to the sofa. She sank back into the cushions with a sigh. "Don't be shy on my account." She patted the empty space beside her. "Sit down."

Jack joined her, taking a swallow before he sat. He glanced at her, trying to gauge her mood. She took a sip of the milk, then closed her eyes.

So far he couldn't read a thing. No wonder she was so good at her job. She'd learned to bury her emotions so deeply, he didn't think even *she* could find them any longer.

She shot him a sideways glance. "Jack, stop worrying about me. I'm fine."

"So you keep saying, but I don't believe you. What you went through tonight doesn't happen every day. You've never been in that kind of situation before."

"And because of that I'm supposed to cower and jump at every strange noise I hear?" Her eyes flew open, flashing with an anger that matched her tone of voice. "Come on, Jack, I have a little more backbone than you give me credit for."

"I don't doubt that for a second," he replied softly. "But I've been in situations where your adrenaline pumps so fast you don't know where to turn next, where you have no control, where there's no turning back."

Wary green eyes searched his, questioning his concern. He knew what she'd see mirrored in his gaze. Worry. Concern.

She leaned forward, placing her mug on the coffee table. Dropping her head into her hands, she rested her elbows on upraised knees and became still as a porcelain statue, delicate and fragile. Moments passed before Jack noticed the slight tremble of her shoulders. A sob escaped her lips soon after.

He gently pulled her into his arms, letting her bury her head against his chest as she succumbed to the wave of delayed shock.

"Shh," he soothed. "It's okay now."

She shook her head, but the sobs continued. Jack waited for the tide of her emotion to ebb. Experience had taught him that it was best to let go completely before dealing with reality.

As she cried, he held her close. Her tears dampened the front of his flannel shirt, but all he thought about was how right she felt in his arms, how her control had finally slipped and she let him share her burden. He rubbed her back in small circles, hoping to relieve her tension. After a moment, he rested his cheek against the top of her head. Her hair smelled sweet and feminine.

He could get used to this.

Minutes passed and finally Teri broke away. He wiped her tears away while she tried an uneven smile. "Thanks."

"Hey, that's what partners are for. Even though you acted on your own tonight, I still consider us a team."

She looked down at her clasped hands in her lap, then back up at him. "How could I have been so stupid?"

He shrugged. "You acted on impulse."

Scooting back onto the sofa, she tucked her legs beneath her, grabbed a throw pillow and clutched it tightly to her chest. "You're right. I got caught up in this mystery." She looked at him, honesty radiating from her. "I really did consider running back to the hotel for help."

Jack leaned back against the cushion. He resisted his longing to hold her again, not wanting her to confuse matters. "If it makes you feel any better, I should tell you that I'd probably have done the same thing."

She grinned. "I know."

"It seems that we both want this mystery solved, pronto."

"Yes, but not at the expense of our lives." She shuddered. "You're right. I must have been nuts."

He chuckled. "Not nuts, just overly enthusiastic. I think that's the real reason you took off after that guy."

Nodding, she traced the floral pattern on the pillow. "It did occur to me that finding out what was going on would look good on my work record." She frowned. "As usual, I put my job first."

Jack stilled her hand and took it in his. "So I guess you learned something tonight?"

She glanced at their hands, then at him. "Ask me that question again tomorrow."

"I will."

"Where have you been all my life?"

"Getting in and out of trouble so that one day I'd be able to give you worthwhile advice."

Laughing, she disengaged her hand from his and leaned back into the cushions.

"How's your arm? Does it still hurt?"

"What arm?" she asked with a sigh.

He chuckled. As she put her head on his shoulder, he gradually sensed her relaxing.

Idly, he stroked her hair, the soft, silky strands threading between his fingers. Her breathing became steady and he knew she had fallen asleep.

Jack, on the other hand, was far from sleep. As Teri slept, he grew more agitated. The enormity of what had transpired tonight haunted him.

In order to regain control, his mind switched into overdrive, running scenario after scenario through his brain. Who had been in the darkened wing? And what would they do now that Teri had discovered them?

He started when Teri mumbled in her sleep. Now that he'd found her, he didn't want someone else to take her away. This wasn't a football game where all he had to do was make the right moves and expect a pass completion. There were too many unknowns here, too many chances for an incomplete pass. Because now, the further into this mystery they ran, the further he carried their lives in his hands.

He stared out the window. Stars winked at him, teasing him with the notion that he was the master of his universe. Yet he never felt less in control than he did at this moment. But he couldn't let Teri know that. She depended on him to help her solve the mystery and keep her job. A job that, in the end, would most likely take her away from him—especially if she learned about his status reports on her.

Why didn't he just tell her? Because he was afraid she'd never trust him again. And that was worse than her leaving because of a transfer.

First thing in the morning he'd get more information. He closed his eyes, taking several deep breaths to wind down his body and mind. Much as he tried, sobering thoughts continued to plague him, keeping sleep at bay.

He was in danger of losing two things: his life and Teri's if he pursued whomever she ran into tonight. If greed was the motive for seeking the jewels, he would be dealing with serious players, especially if the stories surrounding the gems were true.

More importantly, he was in danger of losing his heart. If Teri left West Wind for Paris, she'd take a part of him with her. Because she held his heart in her hands right now and didn't even know it.

He found that danger much worse.

Teri woke with a cramp in her neck and a numb right hand. She tried to move, but her legs were pinned down by a heavy weight. Panicking, her eyes flew open as she prepared to protect herself from whomever had invaded her apartment, only to find Jack's legs over hers, his head resting at the opposite end of the couch.

With one look at Jack she froze. What was he doing here? Suddenly her memory kicked in and the events of the previous night flooded her. Chasing shadows in the dark. Finding that the shadow was indeed a man. Running as if her life depended on it.

Her gaze lingered on Jack's sleeping face. A warmth spread over her as she remembered the most crucial point of the evening: Jack was there for her. To protect her. To dole out comfort and words of advice.

Slipping her legs out from under Jack's, Teri padded into the kitchen to make coffee. She stretched out the kinks in her back, still feeling achy all over. As the familiar aroma of coffee brewing slowly invaded her groggy state, a smile tugged at her lips when she recalled how tenderly Jack had treated her.

She filled two cups and returned to the living room in time to see Jack sit up, rubbing the slumber from his eyes. With his tousled hair and disheveled clothing, he looked extremely huggable.

She tightened her grip on the mugs.

"Sleep well?" she asked.

"No."

"Oh, we're grouchy in the morning."

He shot her the evil eye.

"I see you're not at your best this early." She handed him a mug.

He took it from her. "Are you always this cheery in the morning?"

She smiled. "Yep."

"Great," he mumbled before taking a gulp.

Not wanting to tempt fate, Teri sat on the easy chair beside the sofa. "Thanks for staying with me last night, even though you didn't have to."

He shrugged. "You fell asleep. I had no choice but stay here and make sure you didn't do anything foolish."

"Like I could get into trouble in my sleep."

Grinning, he winked at her. "Had to be sure. Your past actions made it really hard for me to leave. Then you kept talking in your sleep. I didn't want to miss hearing all your deep dark secrets."

"I don't talk in my sleep."

"Are you sure?"

She frowned. "Relatively sure. No one has ever complained before."

Now it was Jack's turn to frown. "Has anyone else ever been given the chance?"

She tried not to laugh at the disgruntled look on his face. "Let me see . . ."

"Teri, don't mess with my head this early in the day."

"Okay. And no, there hasn't been anyone around long enough to hear me talk in my sleep." She looked down into her mug. "If I really do."

Jack yawned and stretched. "I guess we should get ready for work."

She glanced at the wall clock and nodded. "If you want to leave I'll call a cab to take me back to the hotel."

Leaning back into the cushions, Jack put his hands behind his head and closed his eyes. "No, I'll just doze until you're ready."

Placing her coffee mug on the table, she headed for her bedroom. She'd taken one step across the room and stopped. So much had happened between them in such a short time. Suddenly giddy with happiness, she went to him, bending over to kiss the top of his head.

Jack's eyes opened wide, a look of panic passing over his face.

Suddenly self-conscious, she jumped away, nearly

spilling his coffee. "I'm sorry," she whispered, retreating to her room. Before she closed the door behind her, she heard Jack's muffled voice. She rested her head against the door, fighting back hot tears.

So much for acting on impulse. Obviously Jack wasn't thrilled by her impromptu kiss. It broke her heart, but she couldn't let him see her break down again. She had to be tough. Even with him. She had to be strong for her review, just days away.

And soon after . . . Paris.

Chapter Twelve

Once Teri arrived at work, she enlisted the help of her assistant, Tom, to locate the records she needed. Being a history buff, Tom had a good hunch as to where the books might be. He led her to a locked, dank basement in the Gardenia wing, where they quickly located their treasure.

"Tom, will you please stay and help me?" she asked when they returned to her office, arms loaded with crates full of dusty ledgers and guest books.

Tom set the last crate down with a thud. "You want me to stay?"

"Yes, I do. Reading all of this material will take a lot of time, time I can't spare if I do it myself. With your help, we'll be finished much sooner."

Teri quickly set him at ease by explaining exactly what she needed. Tom dove right into the job, eager once he overcame his shyness around her.

Before she started, Teri placed a call to Martin Pressman. She invited him to lunch, hoping he would have some answers to her questions.

An hour passed. Teri read each paper with painstaking thoroughness. She checked dates, then facts about the hotel. Numbers swam before her eyes. One thing became clear: they weren't making any progress.

She sunk into her chair, rubbing her sore arm. "This is more tedious than I thought."

Tom looked up from the page he was studying. "There doesn't seem to be any order to all of this." Clearing his throat, he added. "I know it's not my place, but you look beat. Maybe you need a break. I'll stay here and finish going through the last box."

Teri smiled, suddenly tired and ready for a change of scenery. "You don't mind?"

"No. Actually, I find all this history fascinating."

Rising, she walked around her desk. "Then I'll take you up on that offer. Maybe a walk on the beach will clear my head."

Tom shot her a surprised look.

"Yes, Tom, regardless of what everyone around here thinks, I'm perfectly capable of enjoying a leisurely stroll." Pulling open her bottom drawer, Teri extracted a pair of jeans and a baggy sweatshirt. She kept the spare clothes handy for an occasion like this, although she'd never used them yet. Once dressed, she slipped on a pair of sneakers and headed for the shoreline.

Stepping out onto the sand, she noted that the wind had died down this morning. The beginning of February usually meant that the tourist season was in full swing, but this year the weather had turned unpredictable. Instead of balmy temperatures, the chilly Florida winter stubbornly hung on.

Despite the cooler-than-normal days, Teri enjoyed her brisk walk. She inhaled the crisp salty air, feeling invigorated as the light wind tousled her hair and touched her cheeks. Her mind focused on the beauty around her, instead of the problems at the hotel.

A young couple passed, holding hands as they conversed in hushed tones. Sudden tears prickled behind Teri's lids. How she wished she had someone to share her life with. Even without a mystery, she knew that Jack's presence would have rattled her solitary life. And the more she thought about it, she had to admit that she liked the rush of excitement she experienced whenever Jack was around. He brought out the best in her. And best of all, she liked the fact that they were friends. No matter what happened at West Wind, at least they'd formed a lasting friendship.

After a few minutes of reveling in the quiet of the beach, she realized she must get back to work and strolled back toward West Wind.

As she climbed the cement steps from the beach to the pool deck, she spied a lone figure standing on the far side. Jack. He truly belonged outdoors; his hair shone in the sun, his eyes flashed as he watched her, his tan face seemed to glow with good health. No doubt about it, he stole her heart away.

He strode toward her when she reached the top of the steps. "How's your arm?"

"Sore. Nothing that hard work won't cure. I decided to take a walk to clear my head."

"I'm glad you decided to expend some energy instead of sitting in your office all day."

His serious countenance troubled her. "What's up?"

"Teri, I think we should consider the fact that you might not be safe. If the guys from the other night recognized you, there's a chance they may be back."

Teri's heart went still. "I hadn't thought of that."

Jack shoved his hands into the pockets of his denim jacket. "Someone should stay with you at all times. You need to be extra careful. And you should let me know when you're leaving at night so I can walk you to your car."

"You think I need a baby-sitter?"

"Why not? Isn't it better to be concerned about your safety and take precautions?"

Shaking her head, Teri brushed by him. The review was this weekend. How would it look to her boss if she needed a bodyguard? Someone hovering around her at all hours would disturb her concentration. She had her career to think about.

Besides that, if she admitted she was afraid, her composure would surely be lost. She had to remain strong and deal with the problem. She couldn't botch up another job. "I can't deal with this now. I have an appointment."

"This problem is not going away until we find out who is prowling in the wing and why. You have to deal with it. Is that too much for you to comprehend?"

She stared up into his eyes, unsettled by the fierce emotion she saw there.

"Jack, I can't let anything interfere with my job. I can handle this."

"There was never any question of your lack of ability. You're a successful businesswoman, competent at your work. But being alone could be dangerous given the situation here."

"I don't know," she hedged.

"Just humor me."

"Alright. For now." She glanced at her watch. "Look, I have to change. Martin is meeting me for lunch."

He frowned, about to speak, but she interrupted. "I know how you feel about involving him, Jack, but it's worth a shot."

"Teri—"

"Why don't you join us? Three heads are better than two."

He stood silent for a moment, his eyes shuttered. "I'll see you both in the dining room."

The West Wind restaurant boasted the best food on the beach. In the state. In the entire country, for that matter. A Cordon Bleu chef created culinary masterpieces in the kitchen, while the elegant surroundings in the dining room were a feast for the eye. Soft muted shades of seafoam green and mauve swept over the room in the form of light airy curtains and long full tablecloths. Fresh flowers added vibrant color in the decorative centerpieces. A large crystal chandelier commanded attention as the focal point of the room, while discreet antique gaslights flickered on the walls.

Teri reserved a table by one of the windows overlooking the beach. She and Martin relaxed in tapestry upholstered chairs, sipping coffee.

Martin gazed around the room. "It's been years since I had lunch here with a lovely woman. It still has the same elegance I remember."

Teri smiled, a trace of pride in her voice. "The first day I arrived I thought I'd never seen a more beautiful place. There is such a sense of history here, especially when you think of all the people who have stayed under this roof. So many famous people."

"Such as Capone?"

Teri grinned. "Am I that transparent? Can't I enjoy coffee with a friend without an ulterior motive?"

"I'd believe that were true if it weren't for Mr. Bishop bearing down on us with a intense expression on his face."

Teri looked across the room to find Jack closing the space between them.

The men shook hands in greeting. *It's funny,* she thought, *that while I took Jack's advice and loosened up lately, he only wound himself tighter with worry.*

The waitress returned to take Jack's drink order.

"Why do you have such a fascination with Capone?" asked Martin.

"It's not so much the man himself," Teri said, "it's more the events that took place while he was here. You said they never pinned the jewelry robbery on him, but still the goods were never recovered."

"Why does that interest you?" Martin asked, his astute eyes meeting hers.

"If he stole them, we think he may have stashed them here in the hotel."

"Teri," Jack interrupted. "As security advisor, I have to ask you not to—"

"Jack, please. We need answers, and I think Martin can help." She turned to the older man. "Some strange circumstances have led us to believe that someone else may know about the jewelry. If we could figure out where the objects are, then use them to flush out the culprit, we'd solve the case."

"What a time to turn Sherlock on me," Jack muttered.

Teri glared at him before resuming her questioning. "Do you remember any details? Anything out of the ordinary? Maybe your father mentioned something to you."

Martin rubbed his chin. "Actually, I do recall my father talking about Big Al. That's what they called him. He was bigger than life." Martin chuckled. "I was visiting one day when Al came sweeping through the lobby, wearing his white Fedora and a sharp suit. He always had his entourage with him, along with a woman or two. And when he entertained, he did it with style. He'd take his friends sightseeing in a big black touring car, treating them like family." He lounged comfortably in his chair, obviously enjoying the memories.

"Rumor had it that he came down at the request of the owner, a man he knew from Chicago. He stayed a few weeks, enjoying the weather. My father said he was very generous, especially to the hotel owner's family. They hated to see him leave."

Jack leaned his elbows on the table, suitably interested now. "Did the owner think Capone planned the heist?"

Martin shook his head. "That, I don't know. He didn't confide in my father, but he always proclaimed Al's innocence."

Teri slumped back into the padded chair. "If he isn't guilty, then we're going down the wrong path."

"Not necessarily." Martin took a sip of his coffee, then replaced the china cup in its fine saucer. "What if someone else knew about the robbery?"

Jack grinned. "Like one of Capone's men. Who better to blame it on than their infamous boss?"

Teri frowned. "But then why wasn't the heist ever discovered?"

"Maybe it wasn't meant to be," Martin concluded, a satisfied smile curving his lips.

Teri looked from one man to the other. She wouldn't admit it, but now she was more confused than ever.

"Suppose someone else knew about the robbery," Martin continued. "They hide the jewelry until the police give up, planning to return at a later time. So they conceal the stash. What better place than in a busy hotel, right under everyone's nose?"

Jack brightened. "That's the conclusion we drew. They probably intended to return, but something stopped them."

"I'm still stumped. So what happened next?" Teri asked.

The two men looked at each other and smiled. Jack nodded his head toward Martin and the older man continued with the theory. "Rumors about gangsters and outlaws are a dime a dozen. But suppose this particular rumor was passed down a generation or two. Apparently someone believes the story and has started searching."

"But that doesn't explain why the wing is closed." Teri added, thinking about the perfectly good rooms sitting empty.

"That's true," Jack agreed. "That whole scenario doesn't make sense."

"I'm afraid you'll have to fill me in," Martin said, clearly puzzled.

"When I arrived," Teri began, "the bottom floor of the Jacaranda wing was closed off. The corporation wanted some renovations done. Nothing out of the ordinary there, but the contractor seems to have disappeared, there's been complaints of noises from the guests that we can't find the source of, and no one from corporate has any answers. My superior, Mr. Kramer, is in charge, but hasn't instructed me on a course of action."

"That does seem odd."

"And it gets even weirder. I spoke to a friend of mine at corporate. It seems that someone else is interested in the history of the hotel. She said some of the early records for West Wind were missing, and suggested I look for them here. Since this hotel has strange noises and infamous guests, I thought maybe we'd find some clues. So I have Tom going through the old hotel ledgers now."

"You *what*?" Jack bolted up in his chair. "I thought we agreed to keep this quiet."

Teri gave his arm a patronizing pat. "Calm down. I didn't get real specific, just enough for Tom to look for any strange entries or obvious accounting errors."

Martin looked back and forth at the couple, then said to Jack, "I hope you keep an eye on Miss Price. I think she needs it."

"You've got that right." Jack replied, annoyance in his tone.

Before Teri could get a word in, the waitress served them a plate of finger sandwiches and fruit. Martin dug into lunch with relish. Teri sipped her coffee, forcing herself to sit and politely listen as the two men spoke about the hotel.

They finished lunch and Jack excused himself, leaving Teri to escort Martin to the lobby. Just as he was about to leave, Tom opened the door to her office and called her inside.

"Martin, why don't you come in? Maybe Tom found something."

They walked into the office to find Tom holding an old leather-bound book to his chest and nearly tripping over the chair as he rolled up and down on the balls of his feet with excitement. "You won't believe what I found! Al Capone stayed here in the twenties!"

Teri looked at Martin and grinned. "Yes, we knew that."

Her news didn't spoil Tom's exuberance. He opened the book, brushing the pages with the tips of his fingers until he found a certain page. "He stayed in the Palm Suite in the Jacaranda wing. Wow, this is unbelievable," he said, his gaze never leaving the book.

"What exactly do you have there, Tom?" asked Teri.

Tom tore his gaze away from the page and blinked up at her. "It's an old register. The interesting thing is, that someone made notations about guests in the margins. Do you think they wanted to remember what the guests were like?"

Teri reached out for the book. Tom reluctantly laid it in her outstretched hands. His crestfallen face would have been comical another time, but now she needed answers.

She flipped through the pages as a thought came into her mind. "Martin, why don't you take this home and read through it? You know more about the history here than either Tom or I do. This book might jog your memory about the time period we talked about. Maybe you'll recall something your father told you."

She held it out to him, and he reverently took it, stroking the worn leather. "I'd be happy to read this and tell you anything I know."

As Teri led Martin from the office, he promised to call as soon as possible. She watched him make his way to the car, then turned and strode to Jack's office.

"So, what do you think?" she asked without pre-amble as she entered the room. She halted abruptly when she caught a glimpse of Ed Raven sitting in front of Jack's desk.

"Think about what?" Ed asked. He stretched out in the chair, his boots resting on the oak furniture.

Teri deliberately glared at the boots, then directly at Ed. He quickly set his feet on the floor and sat up straight. "Ah . . . if you'll excuse me, I have to check . . . um . . . something." Rising, he hurried from the room.

Jack tipped his chair back against the wall, his arms resting behind his head. "Do you do that on purpose?"

"Do what?"

"Clear out a room with that look."

"What look?"

"The one that says, 'you are an employee, so don't get too comfortable.' "

"I don't do that."

Jack's brows raised over amused eyes.

"Okay, so I intimidate sometimes. It's my job."

"And you're good at it."

At Jack's flat tone, she didn't know if she should be pleased or justly reprimanded. She clasped her hands together and sat at the edge of the vacant chair, prim and stiff. Just like she had when her boss had reprimanded her at her last job.

The phone rang, breaking the silence as they regarded one another from across the desk.

Jack snatched up the receiver. "Hello? Yes. You're sure? Okay, thanks."

"Hotel problem?"

Looking guilty, Jack stared down at his notes, doodling on the paper. "It's nothing to worry about."

She sensed his hesitation. "Tell me."

Jack glanced up at her. "I had a background check done on Martin."

"What?" She jumped up. "You didn't!"

"Don't get upset. I had to take precautions before I let you confide in the man. For security reasons. Come on, Teri, your job is to run the hotel efficiently, and mine is to do background checks if necessary."

"What you're really saying is that you don't trust my judgment."

He ran his hand through his hair. "Not at all. I have the hotel's best interest at heart. And I didn't want another mark on your record. We have to handle this the right way."

Teri's stomach plummeted. She knew what he implied. It hurt to think that Jack would liken this to the problem at her last managerial post. "Not us. *Me* I know what's at stake, Jack. I want answers as much as you do." She turned and left his office.

"Teri, wait." Jack caught up with her in the hallway. "Don't run from me. I'm concerned about you."

"There's no need. I don't need your help." She turned again, nearly running to her office.

Teri placed her steaming microwave entree on a lap tray and carried it to the coffee table. Plopping onto the couch, she grabbed the remote control, hoping a brainless television show would keep her troubled mind occupied for a while. As she touched the food with her tongue, she burned herself in the process. With disgust, she threw down the fork, clicked off the television and fell back against the cushions, scooping up a throw pillow and jamming it over her head.

She blinked back frustrated tears. Jack's words had hurt her today, but they also scared her. If he thought he had to keep her out of trouble, then how must Kramer see her? Would Jack tell her superiors about the current events at the hotel for the sake of protecting her?

She hugged the pillow to her stomach, squeezing it hard. Sighing, she picked up a framed photo of her father that sat on the end table. *Oh Daddy, what's wrong with my life?* Tears trickled down her cheeks as she ran her finger over the cold glass, tracing the features of his face. No human warmth radiated. Only eyes once filled with life twinkled back at her. If only he were here, advising her in this current disaster.

But there would be no words of wisdom tonight.

Chapter Thirteen

Teri slowed her pace to a light jog, inhaling deep gusts of air. She came to a stop at the seawall of the Intra-coastal waterway and bent over to brace her hands on her knees. With a force of will, she controlled her breathing. Her muscles cried out in agony and her bones ached. Sweat drenched her body, but she ignored it. Her mind ran in another direction.

Don Kramer would arrive later this morning. For the West Wind review.

The mild wind that had tousled Teri's hair when she started her run this morning turned stronger. She glanced up into the ominous sky, watching murky gray clouds swirl above her. Out over the horizon, a heavy black sky signaled the approaching storm. The scent of impending rain permeated the air. Within hours the rains would begin, and if the winds picked up strength over the turbulent Gulf, they'd be in for dangerous weather.

"A perfect day," she muttered with little humor. Working out a cramp in her calf, Teri paced, watching the storm brewing as her stress level heightened. Everyone at West Wind was uptight. A dark atmosphere had formed inside the hotel as well as out here.

This morning's run was supposed to clear her mind, not muddle her brain further. She turned back to the hotel, ready to face Kramer once again.

Rubbing her temples, Teri tried to ease her mounting headache. With the review a matter of hours away, she didn't need the mounting tension of the staff to come to a head today. She stood in the hotel kitchen, listening to the temperamental chef reduce a waitress to tears. And lunch hour hadn't even started.

"Please, Maurice," Teri pleaded. "Cathy didn't mean to criticize your newest creation."

"That's right," Cathy sniffled. "How did I know it wasn't scraps for my dog? You always leave a treat at the end of the counter."

Maurice's shouting, half in English, half in French, rose to new decibels, causing Cathy's shrill wailing to increase. Teri winced. At that precise moment, Don Kramer entered the kitchen.

"Some things, Miss Price, never change."

Teri opened her mouth to explain, but the chef slammed down a pot and bellowed out harsh words while the waitress ran the wrong way out of the kitchen's swinging doors. A loud crash sounded on the other side.

Her boss crossed the room, speaking in French, his placating but firm tones soothing the chef. Kramer's tall, lanky frame sported an ill-fitting suit. He seemed out of place here in a steel-clad kitchen, but to Teri's chagrin, quiet soon reigned supreme. After handling the situation, he strolled back to Teri, a slight curl of his lips marring his face. She noticed small lines fanning from his eyes and gray dusting his hair, new additions since their last visit.

"Let's adjourn to your office to discuss this little episode."

"Right," Teri replied, hoping the crisp tone of her voice would cover her nerves. *Why, why, why,* did this man always catch her at her worst? The scenario had been the same in Daytona—Kramer came sweeping in to correct a problem, then turned formal and condescending. Would she have to put up with his smug behavior again?

As she passed the front desk, Tom gave her thumbs up. *He must think I'm going to an execution,* she thought with morbid humor. *Probably my own.*

Once they reached her office, Teri ushered Kramer into the room, then followed him inside. Passing a mirror, she took a critical appraisal of her appearance. Instead of a severe hairstyle, she'd chosen to soften her features by letting her hair down, pulled away from her face with a fancy clip. Minimal make-up and understated jewelry gave her an air of pleasant authority.

Kramer took the seat behind her desk, momentarily throwing her off guard. Teri tugged her navy suit skirt down and took a deep breath to relax. Of course, his moves were deliberate. But she wouldn't let him get to her.

She viewed her boss, taking in his dispassionate eyes set in a haughty face. His graying brown hair, slicked back in a close cropped style, gave him an air of power.

Something struck Teri as odd about his appearance. Even though Kramer's visit to Daytona had been an emotional whirlwind, she remembered him as being a little more well-groomed, his clothes more designer. It didn't matter though, he was still here to make her life miserable, as only he could.

Realizing Kramer was watching her, Teri cleared her throat. "I have to apologize for that scene in the kitchen. I'm afraid Maurice is passionate about his food. The tiniest remark sets him off."

Kramer shrugged, his shoulders pulling at the dark fabric. "No problem. Guys like that take food preparation too seriously." He picked at a piece of lint on his sleeve. "I'm more concerned about your handling of the situation."

Teri bit her lower lip, trying hard to stay cool. When Kramer didn't continue, she knew he was waiting for her to explain. Or hang herself. "It probably seemed as though things were getting out of hand, but I know from past dealings with Maurice that he needs to vent. You know, part of the artistic temperament. Once he's finished, he usually calms down."

Kramer nodded. "The wait-and-see approach."

"That's right. He'll apologize to Cathy and send her home with a special meal."

"Then I shouldn't be concerned with that less-than-stellar performance I just witnessed?"

Teri seethed. Promotion or no promotion, this man seriously pushed her to the edge! "No, sir. I know my staff and how to deal with them."

Kramer rested his elbows on the arms of the chair and steepled his fingers to support his chin. He stared at Teri for an intense moment, then moved his gaze around the room. "Why don't you have your assistant show me to my room. I'll get settled and we'll deal with business after that."

"Right away." She buzzed Tom and gave him instructions. Once Kramer left, she breathed a sigh of relief.

Glimpsing a streak of light outside, she walked to the window. Black clouds rolled directly overhead. Maintenance workers scurried about, tying up table umbrellas and stacking lounge chairs in preparation of the impending storm.

Teri shivered. On a day like this, she wished she stayed home.

She crossed her arms over her chest and rubbed some warmth into her arms. Resting her cheek against the cool window frame, she tried not to envision the dark future that loomed before her.

She glanced out in time to see the first heavy raindrops splatter the patio and splash into the pool. If it wasn't for the fact that they lived in Florida, she'd expect to see snowflakes. She shivered again, but from the dampness in the air or something else, she wasn't sure.

She paced the confines of her office until she realized she couldn't waste any more time trying to figure out the impossible. Straightening her jacket, she smoothed her hair and headed for the restaurant to reserve a table for an early dinner with Kramer.

As she passed the front desk, Ed sauntered by. He pulled up short when he saw her and a halfhearted smile touched his lips. "Are you looking for Jack?" he asked, his tone almost belligerent.

"No, should I be?"

"You two are usually inseparable." Ed shrugged, his voice tight. "Anyway, I think he had a meeting with Mr. Kramer."

Teri frowned. "Oh? Neither of them mentioned it to me."

"Guess they don't tell you everything."

"No, I guess they don't." Teri tried to reason why Ed seemed so surly with her, but that nagging feeling returned, this time jabbing the pit of her stomach. She excused herself and sought out the hostess.

Returning to the office, she slowly closed the door behind her. She slumped against it, commanding herself to keep breathing deeply.

Why were warning bells ringing when she thought about the meeting between Jack and Kramer? Jack was here to upgrade security, the two men would logically have business to discuss. She couldn't think of any reason they would discuss *her* in particular, but Ed's tone set her on edge. Ed was always cagey, but never disrespectful.

And why didn't Jack deem it necessary to fill her in? Even if their personal relationship was undefined, she still expected a professional courtesy from him. She shook her head. Maybe all the commotion in the wing had him worried. He might not want to make a report on it without conclusive evidence, and Kramer could be difficult to deal with.

That must be it, she decided. *He's reacting to the stress, just like everyone else at the hotel.* She took a deep breath and placed her hand over her beating heart. No need to overreact.

By six o'clock, Teri stood in the foyer, her stomach twisted into vicious knots. She doubted that she'd be able to eat a bite. She glanced at her watch and grimaced. Show time.

She'd brought an outfit from home and changed into a black sleeveless dress, covering her bare arms with a sheer black dress shirt. The color matched her mood. Tonight's meeting would be informal, but she took the time to look her best. One never knew what to expect from her boss.

The dim lights and flickering candles lent a romantic mood to the room, a comfortable contrast to the raging weather outside. But this meeting was anything but romantic—business, and nothing else.

Teri quickened her pace, anxious for this meeting to be over. Kramer stood as she approached. "Please, have a seat, Miss Price."

She sat at the edge of her chair, fingering her pearl necklace. Her boss, dressed in a dark suit, had his hair combed back to perfection and his cold eyes unnerved her. Like the storm outside, her emotions whirled in a frenzy, but she hid her discomfort.

"No need to be nervous. I told you this would be a pleasant dinner."

Teri shuddered inwardly. "I hope your room is adequate?" she asked, making small talk to calm her nerves.

He took a sip from his water glass, then spoke in an even voice. "Everything is fine. You have the hotel running to perfection." He lifted the glass in a mock salute as a waitress hurried to the table, her curious gaze moving back and forth from Teri to Kramer.

"Let's have a bottle of your best champagne," he told the young girl, then waved her off.

"Champagne? Are we celebrating?" *If he's this happy, he must be ready to fire me.*

A slight grin pulled at the corner of his arrogant mouth. "Life is full of celebrations, don't you agree? Tonight is one of them." He chuckled, apparently pleased by his private joke.

Puzzled by his cryptic answer, Teri made an effort to relax, but found it impossible. She anxiously waited for the bombshell Kramer obviously planned to drop on her.

By the time the waitress returned with the chilled bottle and fluted glasses, Teri sat on pins and needles. She accepted the glass Kramer handed to her and stared at her boss.

Kramer's demeanor vaguely resembled the impatient corporate climber she remembered from her last review in Daytona. Could he really be pleased with her efforts here at West Wind?

"Actually, Teri, you're quite gullible."

She nearly choked on the champagne. *Uh-oh,* she thought. *Here it comes.*

The waitress stopped at the table before Kramer could elaborate on his words. Teri ordered the chef's special, sure her flip-flopping stomach would keep her from swallowing a bite.

"I understand you've had some problems with the unused floor of the Jacaranda wing?"

Teri swallowed hard. Judging by the calculating glimmer in Kramer's eyes, she knew her response could make or break her. She licked her lips to speak, her tongue as dry as cotton. "Yes. We had a break-in and the contractor never returned to finish the job. But you know about that, I sent a report to your office."

Kramer poured himself more champagne. "Yes, I remember reading about that. I'm afraid I fired the man."

Teri frowned, confused by his admission. "Why?"

"I had sufficient reason at the time." He held the glass to the candlelight, his eyes mesmerized by the liquid fire reflected inside.

"I wish you had told me. We were very concerned when he never returned."

He raised an eyebrow. "I sent a memo. I see you never received it."

Teri shifted in her seat, acutely uncomfortable with

Kramer's actions. To say that her boss was behaving weird was an understatement.

"But still," he continued, "I didn't receive any reports from you about the break-in."

Teri cleared her throat. "Jack Bishop and I worked together to investigate the incident. Since we hired his firm, he wanted to file the report."

Again, a false smile tugged at Kramer's lips. "Yes, he filed his report. Many, actually. And all very enlightening." He took a sip and continued to gaze at her. "You seem to be the main topic."

"Me?" For a split second, Teri's heart stopped beating. A deep sense of foreboding washed over her. "Why would he submit a report about me?"

Kramer's tone was cold. "For your well-being. You were attacked, isn't that right?"

In her momentary panic, she forgot about the windy night she chased a dark figure into the wing. "It wasn't dangerous." Better to downplay the event. "I saw a trespasser and followed him."

Kramer stared into his drink. "Mr. Bishop seems to think that move was ill-advised."

Her temper heated. "Mr. Bishop wasn't on duty that night. I made the decision alone."

"I see." Kramer leaned over the arm of the chair to retrieve a folder from his briefcase. He casually tossed it to her. She watched it slide, coming to a halt before it slipped off the table. "Go ahead, flip through your file."

With shaking fingers, she lifted the thick folder, mentally bracing herself. She slowly opened the cover.

Her eyes scanned the first page. A report, detailed by Jack, replaying her actions on the first day he arrived. Consecutive pages outlined her work since that day, taking into account her stern interactions with the staff and their unhappy reactions to her. The only words of praise were decisions that affected the guests.

The words blurred and she stopped reading for a moment to peek up from the file. Kramer observed her with an expectant look in his eyes and a smile neatly hidden behind his glass. She looked down quickly, ignoring him. She kept her expression neutral, deciding that she'd rather run naked through the hotel lobby than let Kramer get the best of her again.

When she finished reading, she replaced the papers and handed the file back to him. Her heart felt numb, her mind closed down. She couldn't move, so she waited silently for him to make the next move.

"Nothing to say, Miss Price?"

What could she say to him? That she approved of Jack's spying techniques? That the man she had come to trust implicitly was a fraud? That he most likely befriended her to keep tabs on her? All this might be true, but she would not speak a word of it to him. Or anyone.

Finally he spoke, his tone mocking. "Is there anything our security expert left out?"

She kept her tone light, despite the fact that she was dying inside. "No. It's all there."

He opened his mouth to speak, but the waitress arrived with their meals. Dropping the napkin on the table, Teri rose, unable to stomach the delicious aroma of the food. Waves of nausea hit her with resounding strength. "If you'll excuse me, I'm afraid I'm not feeling well."

Kramer rose. "You do look a bit pale. Why don't you retire to your office and I'll join you after I finish this wonderful meal. After all, we have the future to discuss."

Teri nodded, then fled the room on wobbly legs. As she passed through the lobby, one question tore through her soul, repeating itself over and over as she blindly made her way to the office. *How could Jack betray me?*

Once inside the darkness, she slumped to the carpet, hot tears rolling down her cheeks. Thunder crashed through the silence. Her life flashed before her like lightning: her father's joy when she graduated from college, her disastrous muddle in Daytona, dealing with that episode alone without friends or family for support. And Jack. Always Jack. Smiling at her. Mocking her? She prayed it wasn't so. Her heart had been lonely for so long, but it took Jack's friendship to make her realize what an empty life she'd created for herself.

She finally realized too late that she wanted a family. She missed her father, his absence felt like a physical emptiness inside her. But now she dreamed of a loving husband and children surrounding her, healing that ache with a family's closeness.

She realized she wanted Jack to be that man.

What little they had was a lie. Her fists dug into the plush carpet beneath her. She wished she had the strength to tear it up into great big hunks. How she wanted to destroy something, hurt something, like Jack had done to her dreams. Maybe then the pain that stabbed at her would lessen in comparison.

She wept out her sorrow. This deep–seated anguish would never leave her. She'd given her heart a chance and what did she get in return? Heartache.

She'd lost sight of her original goal, choosing Jack over Paris. To think, she almost let herself believe they might have a chance . . .

Sobbing in her darkened office, she faced her future head-on. Alone and betrayed.

Thunder pounded again, this time almost on top of her. The raindrops struck the window with a violent force. The conditions outside picked up strength while the storm inside her was nearly spent. Her tears slowed and she wiped any vestige of them from her cheeks. Weary to the bone, she lifted herself, smoothing her dress with damp palms. She was a professional, she reminded herself. When all else failed her, she had that fact to fall back on.

Jack entered Teri's dark office. The vibrations from the thunder set his teeth on edge.

She knew. Kramer probably delighted in telling her about the reports, even when Jack asked him not to.

She hadn't noticed him yet. He stepped into the room, silently closing the door behind him just as she flicked on the desk lamp.

"He told you?"

Teri's head jerked up, the surprise on her tear-stained face quickly changing from despair to anger. He deserved that, he thought. Along with a horse whipping.

"What do you want?" she snapped.

"I bumped into Tom. He saw you run into your office and thought I should know."

"Why? So you can write up another report?"

Jack read the pain in her eyes. The pain he caused. Guilt gnawed at him. Her face, so pale in the dim light, accused him. Tortured him.

"Kramer asked me to make those reports on you when I accepted the contract. It was part of the job."

"Some job," she repeated, her voice bitter.

"It *was* just a job, until I got to know you. I won't make excuses, God knows I've made enough of them in my life." He ran his hands through his hair, frustration exploding inside him. "I should have told you, but after we became friends, I didn't know how."

Teri glared at him. "It's simple. You say 'Teri, Kramer asked me to watch you and report back to him.' I say, 'What a jerk,' and we all get on with our lives."

"It's not so simple." He took a deep breath and held it, pushing down the dread that settled on his shoulders. He released the imprisoned air with a gush. "He ordered me not to tell you."

She laughed, lashing out at him. "Oh, well, that explains it. Now it makes perfect sense. You're a principled liar."

"I never lied to you." His words sounded gruff.

"No, but you omitted the truth. You knew how I'd feel about this."

He did know. And he knew the truth would hurt her. That's why he never told her.

She drew in a long breath, then sighed. Her shoulders slumped in what he thought might be defeat. "Get out, Jack."

"We can work this out." He couldn't leave her. Not now.

"Do you have a contract riding on it?"

"Teri, it's not—"

"It doesn't matter." She cut him off with a tight voice.

"Yes, it does."

"You know what's funny, Jack? You always accuse me of putting work first. Of putting my goals ahead of everything else. Well, guess what? We're more alike than you thought."

Chapter Fourteen

The pelting rain matched time to the throbbing ache in Teri's head. Thunder rumbled again and lightning streaked past the window. "What a perfect night," she grumbled.

She sat behind her desk, at a loss of what to do. Her mind refused to concentrate, her body too numb to function normally. So she sat, listening to the storm.

When her phone rang, she ignored it. Then came a brief knock on her door before Tom entered.

"I think we have a problem."

She wanted to laugh. The whole world had problems.

Tom took a deep breath. "With the noises and the review going on, I called your friend Lisa in corporate. I found out that Kramer's been fired."

"What?"

"They let him go yesterday."

A chill skittered down Teri's spine. "Why?"

"I don't know the details. It has something to do with West Wind. Remember you asked me to check on the renovations of the Jacaranda wing?"

"Of course. Didn't he give you the runaround?"

"Yes. Turns out *he's* had all the important files. He hired some guy to look at the property and apply for the permits."

"That must be the contractor Jack saw. But what happened to the permits?"

"Kramer had all the permits, all the records and pertinent information. He must have had an insider working for him. After security searched his office, they found the paperwork you were looking for. And a copy of a letter telling the local guy not to follow through with the renovations."

"But how did corporate find this out?"

"Lisa did some snooping and turned Kramer in. When his superiors asked questions, his answers weren't good enough. Apparently he stormed out of the meeting, telling them they were fools and he didn't need them anyway. I guess that was the last straw."

Teri leaned back in her chair. No wonder she thought Kramer acted strangely tonight. He must have been acting this way for a while, even before his visit. "He came right in here, holding meetings and using his authority to set everyone on edge and we never had a clue."

The same nagging disquiet from earlier in the evening enveloped her again. "Thanks, Tom."

What sort of cruel game was Kramer playing? She

immediately reached out to buzz Jack, then remembered what he'd done. Despite her hurt feelings, she needed to let him know what she learned.

Jumping up, she left the room, her determined paces taking her to Jack's office. The room was empty. She turned to leave, but the fax machine clicked on. Curiosity stirred through her. With all she'd been through tonight, reading Jack's message was last on her list of no-no's.

The page printed out and she took it from the tray. It showed a sketchy image of an old arrest record. She scanned the text quickly. One name jumped off the page when she read it. *Kramer.*

When the police couldn't pin the theft of the jewelry store on Capone, they managed to find a scapegoat. A man by the name of Leon Kramer. Address: Chicago. A note following the report stated that he was one of the men visiting an upscale hotel with Mr. Capone and had been seen in the vicinity of the store the night in question. Though there wasn't enough evidence to hold him, the local police made the arrest anyway. Capone retained a lawyer and had the man released on false charges. As far as surveillance records went, Kramer left with Capone days later. End of story.

Not so, Teri's mind screamed. She didn't believe this was a coincidence. Not with all the information and events coming together.

She grabbed the fax paper and ran to the front desk. "Where's Jack?"

A puzzled frown crossed Tom's face. "I haven't seen him since he left your office."

"If you see him, tell him to find me *immediately!* You got that?"

She barely heard his reply as she burst into her office, stopping short when she found Kramer inside, standing beside her desk. Papers were strewn all over the floor. She swallowed hard, anger gripping her, but she stood her ground, focusing on him more clearly. His styled hair was mussed and wet. From the rain? His eyes gleamed, as if holding a secret he refused to share with anyone.

"Can I help you?" she asked, grateful that her voice sounded normal.

"Do you know how long I've dreamed of this day?"

Teri crushed the paper in her hand and shook her head.

"A very long time," he continued. "Years, in fact."

"Why is that?"

"Don't play coy with me. I know that you and Bishop have been searching for the jewelry."

Teri opened her mouth to reply, but just as quickly closed it. Kramer was losing it. Nothing she said would matter to him.

"My grandfather told me about the jewels. Just before he died last month, he gave me the final clue. He'd been holding out, afraid to reveal the depth of his secret. But time was on my side." His eyes were shadowed in a clouded daze, but held no hint of pleasure.

Teri eased her way to the door, grabbing the knob with her damp hand, only to feel it turn at the same time. The door swung open, hitting Teri in the hip.

Ed stuck his head in, nudging his glasses onto the bridge of his nose. He forced the door wider, knocking Teri away from the only means of escape. Noticing her, he quickly stepped inside the room and shoved the door shut.

"Don?" Ed hovered near, not taking his eyes off her. When he addressed her boss on a first-name basis, she quickly realized whose side he was on. Ed was the insider.

With that revelation, her heart sank.

A clap of thunder reverberated in the room. Goose bumps needled up and down Teri's thinly clad arms. She dropped the ball of paper and clenched hands at her side, afraid to move, not sure how her movements would affect either of them.

Kramer's cold eyes pierced hers. Teri backed up as far as she could, bumping into the wall behind her.

"Where are they?" he demanded, taking a few steps toward her.

Her dry tongue stuck to the roof of her mouth. "I don't know."

Kramer shook his head and spoke to Ed. "Take her down to the wing. She'll show us."

Ed frowned, still frozen in place. "Are . . . are you sure? Her staff will miss her."

Kramer stared through him. He spoke, his voice low and menacing. "I'll think of a good reason to keep them busy." He jerked the door open and left.

Teri released a tightly held breath. She glanced at Ed, but he fumbled for something in his pocket. "Ed, you don't have to do this. We'll call Jack."

"No." He extracted a pocketknife. She jumped back, her eyes riveted on the shiny blade. "Keep quiet."

She backed away, hoping space and reason would stop him. "Why are you doing this? Kramer's insane. Do you think he'll let you go after he finds what he's looking for?"

"Don's my uncle," he hissed at her.

She froze with terror as he lunged forward, grabbing her arm to spin her around before he jerked her close.

Jabbing the blade to the small of her back, Ed squeezed her arm and led her to the front desk. "Hey, Tom. Miss Price is going to surprise Jack with dinner, so you can handle anything that comes up."

Tom looked at Ed's hold on Teri, then to her face. "Are you sure?"

Ed twisted her arm savagely. She winced, but refused to speak. He twisted harder and she went limp with the pain. "Yes," she said through pursed lips. "It's a surprise."

Tom frowned "But . ."

"She's sure," Ed cut in.

Before she could say anything else, Ed pushed her down the hallway. She turned and mouthed the words, *Call Jack*. Ed jerked her again and Teri lost her footing. Her ankle turned and she almost fell. "Slow down."

"Shut up." Ed pushed her through the door and out into the storm. Pelting rain struck her like stinging needles. They ran to the entrance of the wing, stepping into the gloomy stairwell. A bright light flashed as lightning struck. Shivers ran down Teri's spine.

When they reached the door to the wing, Ed released his grip on her arm and fumbled with the flashlight. "I hate this place," he muttered. "Don always wants it dark down here." Finally he pressed the switch on. The knife blade shone in the arc of light and, with morbid curiosity, she stared, until Ed's words penetrated her mind.

"Where you the one down here searching the walls?"

"Yeah. It's funny. You and Jack were trying to figure out what made the noises, and it was me all along. Some ghost I am. It was all I could do to keep from laughing out loud when Jack told me you were going to stake out the guest room."

Another onslaught of shivers attacked Teri. With the tip of Ed's knife pointed at her, she didn't dare rub her arms for warmth.

A male voice came from one of the rooms down the hall. Ed pushed her toward the sound and over the threshold. A lantern, set on the floor, cast a somber glow over the room. After getting her bearings, she realized Ed had brought her to the room she'd hidden in the night she followed the intruder. Then she realized that Jack stood before her, surprise registering on his face.

"Teri, what are you doing here?"

She tried running to him, but Ed dropped the flashlight and grabbed her collar to hold her back. She jerked as the material dug into her neck, leaving her choking and gasping for air.

Jack leaped to her aid.

"Don't touch her, Bishop." A voice came from the doorway.

Ed jerked her away from Jack's grasp. They all turned. Shadowed in the hallway stood Kramer, a pistol pointed at her head. "Now let's be civilized. Stay calm everyone."

Teri heard Jack's furious breath expel behind her. Ed's hold on her loosened marginally as his hands trembled. It seemed even he didn't know what to expect tonight.

"Uncle Don, this doesn't seem right."

"Just do as I say." Kramer waved the gun, ushering them to the back of the room. Ed still held her but she decided not to fight. Now wasn't the time to infuriate Kramer any more than necessary. She glanced at Jack and saw the questions reflected in his eyes, before Ed turned her away.

A motion caught her attention and out of the corner of her eye she noticed Jack inching closer. She held her breath, praying that Kramer was too preoccupied to notice.

"The jewels aren't here," said Jack.

Kramer glared at him through slitted eyes. "How do you know?"

Jack shrugged. "We've searched all these rooms top to bottom. You don't think you're the only one who knows about the hidden cache, do you?"

Kramer looked confused for a moment. "No one else knows about this. I'm the only one."

"Sorry." Jack shifted his stance. "Someone let the cat out of the bag."

"There's no one else," Kramer bellowed, but uncertainty laced his tone.

Teri's heart hammered as Kramer slightly lowered the gun.

"My grandfather told me about the jewels. He swore no one else knew. He promised I'd find them and I'd be rich. It was his legacy."

"Did he mention he had an accomplice?" Jack asked.

"No," Kramer growled. "He swore no one knew." He grew more agitated and pointed the gun at Teri's chest. "Search this room, Ed."

Ed immediately released his grip and Teri rubbed her aching arms, trying to massage some feeling back into her weary limbs through damp clothing.

"Don't move, Bishop, or I swear I'll shoot your lady."

Teri's gaze traveled to Jack and their eyes met. She read raw determination there. She shook her head, afraid he might do something rash. He returned her smile, a melancholy twist to his lips. Her heart lurched and she realized she loved Jack, would love him always. No matter what he'd done, she couldn't ignore the heaviness in her heart when she imagined life without him.

"There's nothing here," Ed complained. "Jack's right. I followed them down here every time they came. They never found anything."

Jack's gaze narrowed on Ed.

"That's right," Teri explained. "Ed was behind the

noises. I'm sure he was following Kramer's instructions."

"That's not important now," Kramer snarled. "Just keep looking." He brushed his hand through his hair, the ends standing straight up in disarray. His crumpled suit looked pitiful compared to its earlier pristine condition. Kramer didn't wear frustration well.

"He's been behind this from the beginning," Teri continued, ignoring Kramer, even as his face turned fiery red with each word she spoke. "He fired the contractor, but kept the permits so we'd be confused. He sent Ed to make the noises."

Kramer glared at her. "He had access. I planted him here for information."

Jack nodded at Ed from across the room. "Now I understand your interest in what we were doing here in the wing."

"Enough talk," Kramer shouted. "Keep working or I'll shut you up. Permanently."

Judging by the crazed expression on his face, Teri had no doubt that he meant it. She didn't want to imagine just how he'd silence them.

She struggled to remain upright when a wave of fatigue hit her. Leaning back against the wall, she winced when her sore arm touched the hard barrier. As she rested, she noticed another shadow move out of the darkness. She squinted, sure her imagination was running wild in this stressful situation. But still the dark form crept closer. Shifting to get a better look, she lost sight of the movement.

"Stand still, Miss Price, or I'll have to subdue you."

Kramer clicked his tongue in disgust. "I should have taken care of you the night you foolishly decided to play detective."

"That was *you*?" Teri's stomach swam with nausea.

"Of course." He looked directly into her eyes, a flash of admiration lingering there. "I never expected so much gumption out of you. Even so, you don't think I'd trust Ed to carry out this job." His attention shifted to his nephew. "Keep searching!"

Teri watched Ed's progress, her mind numb. She never dreamed Kramer could be the man who assaulted her that night. But then why would she? He'd turned out to be a pro at covering his tracks.

A prickly sensation at the back of her neck set off alarm bells in her mind. She peered over Kramer's shoulder, but the shadow had disappeared again. *I'm losing it*, she thought.

"You can't believe that after all these years the jewels would still be here?" Jack baited Kramer and the man grew more agitated.

"I never knew my grandfather as a child. He lived most of his life in prison for a crime he didn't commit. As he grew older, he summoned me, telling me stories of the old days. His clues were clever, but I figured them out." Kramer frowned. "The jewels are here. Find them!" he screamed again.

Teri looked at Jack, but his eyes were trained on the door. She glanced at Kramer and saw the shadow again. The murky light revealed little, but this time the form held what resembled a shovel. It raised in the air and came crashing down on Kramer's head. Jack jumped Ed, forcibly restraining the younger man.

Teri watched in stunned disbelief as Kramer fell, the gun dropping out of his grasp. To her surprise, Martin walked out of the darkness, a sheepish smile on his face.

"I hope I didn't hit him too hard," he said, gazing down at the limp form at his feet.

A muffled curse turned Teri's attention away from the weapon to Jack. A scuffle ensued as Ed turned on Jack. The two men crashed into the wall, and like a slow motion picture frame, the drywall crumbled away, swallowing the men into a dark hole. They landed with a thud, moans escaping both of them.

Teri ran to Jack's side, anxious for his safety. "Jack, are you okay?"

Martin rushed up behind her, shovel poised, ready to help.

"Yeah, I think so."

"Get me out of here," Ed whined, still pinned under Jack.

Teri and Martin grabbed hold of Jack's arms, pulling him up from the collapsed wall. Ed cried out as Jack's weight eased off him. "Ow. I think my ribs are broken."

Jack climbed safely out of the rubble, leaving Ed laying on the floor cradling his side, rocking and moaning. Once Jack stood on steady feet, Teri threw herself into his arms. She held him tight, inhaling his masculine scent, savoring his closeness. He searched for her lips and she returned his kiss, thankful that he wasn't hurt.

She gently broke the embrace. "I was so afraid," she whispered, her hands cupping Jack's scraped face.

He ran his hands in her hair, over her skin. "You're safe now."

Teri held Jack's face until Martin's muffled voice interrupted her. "I think you'd better see this."

With his arm around her shoulders, Jack led Teri to Martin, who knelt before the hole, the upper half of his body hidden inside. After a moment, Martin sat back on his heels and he drew out a dusty blue jeweler's bag.

Awed silence filled the room, broken only by a loud crack of thunder.

"Open it," Teri whispered.

Martin loosened the drawstring, then dumped the contents into his hand. Ed moved closer now, forgetting his injury long enough to grab a flashlight and shine it on their discovery.

Teri gasped as, one by one, different pieces of jewelry dropped from the bag, the magnificent gems sparkling in the beam of light. Deep sapphire blue, rich emerald, blood red ruby, and sparkling amethyst. Each designed as a masterpiece of its own.

"Beautiful," Martin breathed.

Jack picked up a ruby and diamond bracelet, the stones flashing fire between his fingers. "No wonder Kramer wanted this."

"And still does."

Teri felt a twist on her arm and the pistol dug into her shoulder blades. "Hand over the bag."

Teri nearly fell over at the sound of Kramer's voice. She looked up to find him poised over the group, brandishing the gun she'd neglected to pick up in all the excitement. How could she have been so careless?

"I said, hand them over."

Jack gathered up the treasure and stiffly rose to hand the bag over.

"Ed, escort Miss Price to my car. I'll take care of these two."

"*No!*" Teri screamed, edging closer to Jack. She tasted her fear as Kramer's intent sunk into her brain. She couldn't let Kramer kill any of them now.

Ed hesitated. "Don't you think we've done enough? We got the stuff, now let's get outta here."

"We need Miss Price as a precaution. You don't think I'd leave any witnesses, do you?" He waved the gun at Teri. "Take her. Now."

Teri hung onto Jack until Ed pried her fingers loose. Jack made no move to stop him. His eyes never left the gun. She kicked and screamed, but Ed managed to pull her away. Despite his claim of sore ribs, his grip was as strong as ever.

Through her tears she saw Martin next to Jack. Ed dragged her through the door and they disappeared from her sight.

"Stop fighting me," Ed grumbled.

Teri continued her struggle. "How can you go along with this? Can't you see he's using you?"

"No, he's not. He needs me." He yanked her arm

back until she cried out in pain. "Not like Jack. He never needed my help. Besides, Don won't do anything stupid."

"He'll kill them," she snapped.

"Come on." He curved his free arm around her waist and tried to lift her, but her writhing kept him from getting a firm hold. Abandoning that strategy, he tightened his hold on her arm.

He shoved her into another empty room, pushing open a sliding door. The curtains flew up in the wind and rain pelted them with its gale force. Lightning lit the night sky, and a deafening clap of thunder followed in its wake.

Teri dug her feet into the carpet in one last attempt to stop Ed. "Why are we going out this way?" she yelled over the roar of the storm.

"I don't want anyone to see us leave." He crushed her waist, trying to lead her resisting body outside. "Quit struggling and let's go."

Just before Ed yanked her completely out the door, Teri heard a gun shot. Her heart froze in her chest.

The parking lot lights were obscured by sheets of rain. Raising her hands to shield her face, Teri resisted as Ed dragged her toward the cars.

Her ears filled with the storm's fury. She twisted and fought, but Ed yanked her forward. He stopped to pull out his keys and Teri jammed his shin with the heel of her pump.

He cursed but held on tight, fumbling with the keys as he held onto her struggling body. Just as he opened the door and tried to push her inside, Teri reared back and kicked his shin in the same place, this time harder. Ed roared, and his hold on her went slack. With all her might, she shoved him into the side of the car. He lost his balance. Teri turned and sprinted toward the main entrance. She looked back once to see Ed's car wheels spinning as he raced out of the parking lot.

Just before she reached the door, Jack ran out, sliding to a stop before her.

"You're not dead!" she cried, throwing her arms around him as tears streamed down her cheeks. "I thought you'd been shot."

"Not a chance," he answered. "I told you I'd take care of you and I meant it."

Pulling back, she cast him a trembling smile as she touched his wet face, her fingers brushing lightly over a scratch. Running her hands over his soaked chest, her eyes narrowed when she saw the ripped material. "You look like you've been through a war," she whispered.

With a curse of impatience, Jack dragged her into his embrace.

They were both alive. And drenched to the skin.

After long silent moments, Teri leaned back, brushing her tangled hair from her face. "Is Martin okay?"

He smiled. "Just fine. I stopped Kramer from using the pistol on either of us. He should be waking up with a headache about now."

She took a shuddering breath.

Jack ran his finger gently over her cool cheek. "He'll pay for what he's done."

"I know." Suddenly she started to shake. Jack wrapped her close to him, kissing her forehead in reassurance. Seconds passed before he placed his lips over hers.

"Everything will be fine," he whispered against her mouth.

Sirens blared in the distance, growing louder as the police raced to the hotel. Right on cue the rain slowed, as if someone had turned down a spigot. The parking lot lights burned brighter now. The wind continued to blow, but with less severity than minutes before.

Jack pulled his lips from hers and stared into her troubled eyes. "I think the storm is finally over."

"Maybe the storm, but not the problems." She blinked. "To think, all this time the jewels were really here. How did you know?"

"Martin called me earlier today. He agreed that the jewels must be hidden in the building; it's the only thing that made sense. He drove to the hotel and we went on a hunt."

"Those jewels are worth a fortune."

Jack watched her, his eyes bright with emotion. "The only important jewel in my life is you. And I intend on keeping it that way."

"I'm glad you feel that way, Jack, but you hurt me. I don't know if I can forgive you."

Chapter Fifteen

Jack paced the confines of his office for the tenth time, hands jammed deep into his pockets. Where was she? It had been three days since that fateful night. Once the police arrived, they were separated in the chaos and he hadn't seen Teri since.

The telephone to her apartment rang, but she didn't answer. He learned that she'd taken a leave of absence and, knowing her work habits, that didn't ease his anxiety. Martin claimed ignorance to her whereabouts and Tom, suddenly acting like a mother hen, refused to reveal his saintly boss's location—or to relay Jack's messages.

A rush of dread stopped him mid-pace. He'd never felt this out of control, so unable to fix a mess. If he couldn't find Teri, he couldn't apologize, couldn't beg her forgiveness on bended knee.

He went to Teri's office, leaning against the door

177

frame to stare inside. Memories of time spent with her assaulted him, bittersweet in the aftermath of his actions. An unfamiliar tightening of his throat overwhelmed him and he escaped to another part of the hotel.

He missed her. Desperately. He'd made the ultimate mistake of his life and it cost him his heart.

Unless he could make things right.

"He's worried about you," Martin said as he lowered himself into the patio chair next to hers. Teri smiled at him, her heart cold and heavy.

"You didn't tell him I was here, did you?"

Martin patted her hand with his. "As much as I think you're making a mistake, no, I didn't tell Jack."

She sighed, fatigue washing over her. Between the events of that dreadful night and the non-stop questioning from the police these past few days, Teri needed to relax. She'd escaped to Martin's home, seeking refuge to lick her wounds. The hurt, so fresh and new, threatened to never leave her.

The soft breeze gently lifted her hair. Sitting on Martin's back porch in the warm March sunshine did little to lift her spirits. Even Martin's sunny disposition couldn't revive her mood. "I need a few days to unwind."

He nodded in understanding. "You're welcome to stay as long as you'd like."

Teri stared out over the sparkling water. She didn't know how long she'd stay, or even if she would stay. Right now her mind was fuzzy and she couldn't think clearly. Until this state of confusion passed, she'd be content to sit on the wooden porch and simply stare off into the incredibly blue sky.

Later that day, as twilight streaked across the evening sky in shades of orange and purple, the sun made its final descent of the day. Teri strolled along the shore, seeking refuge in the elements.

She'd grown to love it here. The secluded beach offered sanctuary. Here, she could wiggle her toes in the cool, wet surf, instead of answering questions for the police, the corporation, and Jack.

Jack. As usual, her thoughts returned to him. Nothing seemed to keep her mind off of him. She loved him. She just had common, day-to-day problems like betrayal and hurt to deal with.

Raising her hands above her head, she stretched out the kinks of tension. A warm breeze fanned over her knit shirt with the hotel insignia embroidered on the pocket. Teri hunkered down to sift through a pile of shells when she heard a noise behind her. Turning her head, she caught a glimpse of Jack silhouetted in the setting sun. Her heart leapt, but residual anger made her words harsh. "What're you doing here?"

He grinned. "Just out for a walk."

"Here?"

He shrugged. "I know the owner. He won't mind."

She stood and regarded him for a moment, struck by how handsome he looked in old jeans and a T-shirt, his feet bare. He fit into the elements so well; rugged and strong.

"Digging for treasure?"

"Please, one treasure in sixty plus years is enough for me." She couldn't help but notice how naturally she slipped into the easy camaraderie between them, even though she was still angry.

"Corporate is pressing charges. I guess Kramer got more than he bargained for."

"Greed must have made him snap." Teri shivered, just thinking about him. Deep inside she had always sensed Kramer's vicious character. From the first time she met him, she sensed his wickedness. He enjoyed taunting her, first in Daytona, then at West Wind.

Jack reached out to brush her hair behind her ear, his fingers grazing her cheek. She wanted to push him away, telling him she'd never trust him again, but instead stared up at him.

"When Ed brought you to the wing, I was never so scared in my life. When I think what might have happened . . . if Kramer had pulled the trigger . . ." His fingers lingered in her hair.

Teri swallowed past the lump in her throat. "It's over now. All of it."

He removed his hand and shoved it in his pocket. "All of it?"

Good question. How could she let him off the hook for what he'd done? "Why didn't you tell me about the reports?" she whispered.

He closed his eyes for a second, then straightened his shoulders. "I tried. Once." He shifted his stance. "At first it was a job. I owed the corporation since Marcus took a chance on me. I didn't know you then. I'd heard about problems at the Daytona property, so at the time, I didn't think Kramer's request for reports were unreasonable."

"I read them, you know." Her voice turned brittle. "Not exactly glowing."

"In the beginning you rubbed me the wrong way. You rubbed *everyone* the wrong way. You barked orders, expecting perfection all the time.

"But after we spent time together and we got to know each other, I couldn't decide if I should tell you. It got harder every day, especially with the review looming. I didn't know how you'd take it." He shrugged. "I guess I thought I could take care of everything but it backfired on me."

Teri paced a few steps and turned her back to Jack, trying to control the wayward emotions that reeled whenever she was with him.

"So what am I supposed to do now? Forget the fact that you betrayed me? That you didn't think enough of me to tell me the truth?"

He came up behind her, so close she could feel his breath in her hair. "I knew this job meant *everything* in the world to you. If you thought I was a threat to your job security, you would have dropped me in a minute. Then where would we have ended up?"

She sighed, her shoulders sagged. "Right where we are."

He placed his hands on her shoulders and gently turned her around. His smile, soft and heartfelt, melted the last of her reserve. His eyes grew dark. "I'm sorry for the pain I caused you. I wouldn't intentionally hurt you for the world."

Teri's heart beat wildly in her chest, and the gloom that hung over her for days blew away with the breeze. "You're right about one thing," her voice quaked with emotion. "I was hard on the staff. All I talked about was the promotion and Paris. How I wanted to be the next rising star. I'm surprised you even bothered with me."

"It had to be love," he teased.

"Excuse me?"

"I love you."

At his words, Teri realized that the job she'd held so important in her life was only that, a job. Jack was her life, and with him she'd find happiness that would last a lifetime.

She threw her arms around his neck, determined never to let go. He loved her! Her dreams were coming true and she'd almost blown it over pride.

"I love you, too," she whispered against his ear.

"I know."

She pulled back, slightly annoyed by his cocky grin. He lowered his head to her, his lips brushing hers in the sweetest rush. She cupped his face and deepened the kiss.

He hugged her in a bold embrace, then lifted her into his arms. "I suggest we go somewhere more private to discuss our future."

"Future?" She wrapped her arms around his neck and couldn't stop smiling. "What did you have in mind?"

"How about a trip? Just the two of us. With everything that's been going on, you deserve a break from the hotel."

"Umm, I like the way that sounds." She kissed him again until he broke away, laughing.

"We'll never get to making our plans if you interrupt me."

"Don't worry. I'm sure I can come up with a suitable vacation spot. After all, I'm in the resort business."

He shook his head. "Nope. The destination is already taken care of."

Her brows rose in puzzled surprise.

"Get the envelope out of my back pocket."

Reaching around his hips, Teri grabbed hold of the thick envelope.

"Go ahead. Open it."

In the last dying rays of light, Teri pulled out a set of airline tickets and read the destination. She smiled up at him, her heart warm with love.

She'd get to Paris after all.